Some Assembly Required

Some Assembly Required

Michael Strelow

ROUNDFIRE BOOKS

Winchester, UK
Washington, USA

First published by Roundfire Books, 2017
Roundfire Books is an imprint of John Hunt Publishing Ltd., Laurel House, Station Approach, Alresford, Hants, SO24 9JH, UK
office1@jhpbooks.net
www.johnhuntpublishing.com
www.roundfire-books.com

For distributor details and how to order please visit the 'Ordering' section on our website.

ISBN: 978 1 78535 627 8
978 1 78535 628 5 (ebook)
Library of Congress Control Number: 2016958229

A CIP catalogue record for this book is available from the British Library.

Design: Stuart Davies

Printed and bound by CPI Group (UK) Ltd, Croydon, CR0 4YY, UK

Chapter I

Of all the things you can imagine in the world—there are even more.

First let me tell you about the voices—no, the storm outside. No, the voices first. In some ways, the same things. The storm is full of voices; the voices full of storms. But that's way ahead of myself.

My voices have always pointed out the world to me. They never told me to do things—good things or bad things. No fiend in my ear with an evil agenda and no religious ecstasy with the privilege of God's command. A voice would say, "Watch what the sun does just as it disappears over the horizon." Or, it would point out the river surface, how it rippled up the poplars and broke the greens and yellows into shards. The voices sometimes (my personal favorite) out of a quotidian silence would suddenly just say, "Jake." Maybe they were only fooling around. Turns out there's a lot of *only fooling around* that goes on in the world.

But a voice would do that. And then nothing. Never did it say to kill so-and-so or drown puppies or let the air out of the neighbor's tires. Never. As complicated as the voices ever got, before Rex that is, was blathering to me about the violet color necessary to paint that cloud-gray color on a fall afternoon. The voices came out of what I was thinking, it seemed, but not part of the thinking, just invited by the thinking. They were clear and separate and suddenly there like a voiceover, like sudden attention. *Blah, blah, blah*. They said, *blah, blah, blah.*

And I always respected the blah. At first I didn't know any better. I don't really remember how it came up, but I must have been about five or six. I mentioned the voices to an adult (I figured everybody had them), and suddenly there was a shit storm around me that included my teacher, some professional counselor at the school, my parents and even the interrogation of my friends. "Those voices," they'd ask me, "do they ever . . . you know . . . ask you to . . . want you to DO anything? Do you want to hurt yourself?" Finally, I convinced everyone that the voices just went away. They just stopped I guess, I told them. Maybe there weren't *really* any voices after all, I said; I might have just been talking to myself. Everybody talks to themselves, don't they? "And how are we today?" the counselor was fond of greeting me. "I'm fine," I replied with singular emphasis. *"I'm* just fine." I had realized at this young age that not everyone heard the voices. And it also became clear that my job as a young man would be to figure out just what part of my world I shared with everyone else, what parts were mine alone.

This voices business. I learned later, of course, that this is a very old epistemological problem: what is there we can know? And how do we know it? It's the next questions, though, that grabbed me by the ass very early on, earlier than if I had had no voices, I think. *Who else knows what we know*? And all the corollaries: who else knows stuff we can never know? That one has kept a circus of philosophers very busy. I think philosophers come in the quantity of one circus, two circuses, three or more circuses. The voices, I now believe, made me a philosopher at a very young age. I learned to be discursive. All adults questioning me about the voices gave me a chance to try out my interrogation judo. Whatever anyone was looking for, they would not find. Looking for voices? Find no voices. Looking for how that makes me feel? Find I don't own that feeling at all. Look for a troubled young man? You must find a young man of great joy and good humor. This strategy worked for a while only. I made it through my twenties using this judo. But the coming of Rex blew up the whole counterpunching enterprise.

But for a while the dodging was lots of fun. Almost everyone in the shit storm I unleashed on myself by first copping to the voices was earnest . . . and thoughtful . . . and solicitous . . . and, finally, in my humble opinion, for some reason shallow and silly.

It seemed I had somehow collected all the soft-brains in my locale and called them down on my poor self. Voices? I should say not! Voices? You should also say not. Just own the fuckers and get on with your life. They're just extra wiring, I came to think. I got a little bonus in the neuron tangle that makes it seem like someone's jabbering at me. Big deal. In the wild, I probably would have been a shaman and claimed all kinds of god-contact. Later, I found one investigator of consciousness, Julian Jaynes, who claimed that 3,000 years ago *everyone* heard voices. Before the development of what he calls the modern mind, all of us wandered around hearing voices, having visions and waking dreams. And now there are organizations like Hearing Voices Network (HVN) and Intervoice, the international equivalent (big convention of hearers in Paris this year), organizations for all the people who hear voices that aren't mental illness.

Powerful shit in the wild, those voices. In the second grade, not so much. So I dodged—fake left, go right.

And so, I was . . . just fine. As long as, I had learned well, I never mentioned the voices again, nor any of that business, as Macbeth's witches say, "by the prickling of my thumbs, something wicked this way comes." Marnie and I had been together for three years before I opened the subject. I thought I'd start out from pretty far away and test the water.

"I read today that St. Thomas Aquinas had ten proofs of the existence of God. And one of them was hearing voices in our heads, you know, the way we talk to ourselves. He figured that we were made essentially double—God and ourselves in one package. And the talking to ourselves part . . . that was God keeping channels open or something like that." Insert pause here. Thumb magazine. "So do you ever, you know, hear voices?"

I was, of course, just making shit up. Aquinas had five ways, not ten. He never really mentioned voices. But he could have, given the nature of the five ways that prove God's existence.

"Yes," she said, fully aware that I made shit up. "And they

keep telling me to murder you in your sleep." Casually then. "But I never do, do I?"

Marnie was as funny as she was beautiful. She knew funny. Good thing, too. It would prove to be essential to everything. Without funny, many mistakes would have been made, many unnecessary mistakes regarding Rex. Many things would have gone terribly wrong—or at least wrong-er. She sat on the couch looking over at me as if the topic of murdering me in my sleep were closed. Over and done. Not so fast. She pulled back her beautiful dark hair. I know for a fact she never used conditioner. And still it shone.

"Yeah, but . . ." I continued. "But do they tell you how you should do it, the murder? Like what to use, what to do with the body afterward? Do they—are there more than one?—do they want any kind of ritual with it? And garbage disposals? Any mention of . . . ?" Flashback to my youthful voices interrogation. I laugh now, but in those days my voices seemed to be on the mind of every adult around me. It was as if they got together each day and contrived to make a group effort to root out my irregularity and interrogate it out of existence. Those solicitous wide eyes as they waited for reports on my voices, the hand patting my arm, rubbing my shoulder in sympathy—I wanted to scream: NO VOICES NOW. BIG FUCKING MISTAKE TELLING YOU IN THE FIRST PLACE! LEAVE ME ALONE. But, of course, I would never. I laugh now about the "middle way" claimed by the Buddha, *my* inner Buddha. All that excess and ado and bad proportion that the middle way would mitigate, all the jackass moves and thoughtless shooting from the hip I could have avoided if I'd really made my voices go hide out in a cave. Not so easy a thing, it turns out. Rex, the voice of thunder, my Loki and coyote trickster there sitting on my shoulder though I could deny and deny and deny.

Marnie, dipped in droll, went on. "Not garbage disposals. Not exactly anyway." She had one leg folded up under herself, one sock on the coffee table. And that's how she always pulled it off. Casual elegance while intoning the most thoroughly outrageous twaddle thrilling my inner twelve-year-old that shared space with my inner Buddha. She said, "They're kind of foggy about the details, but there's some kind of grinder thing involved or maybe an ore crusher of some kind. Anyway, a big sucker. More like a big blender maybe, but I've never seen a blender this size. And the way they want me to hack off . . . well, I've said too much already. I really don't listen to them, like I said."

And she went back to her magazine. It was fully two minutes before the smirk let me know how pleased she was with herself.

"Remind me not to play poker with you," I said. And the subject was closed. Temporarily, as it turned out.

Marnie was a lady but not so much that she couldn't pull off the murder-you-while-you-sleep thing. That was one of the cool parts of the whole package. Whatever appeared in her right hand would have its balance appear in her left. All her yin worked a little yang too. She did things with her hair as she read as if she were inventing a hairdo to go with the text; she twisted and coiffed and plumped with her free hand. Turn the page, then twiddle and flick and pull hair away from her head. I watched her and thought she might be trying out antenna formulae. The poet Theodore Roethke had a poem about a woman "lovely in her bones." Marnie was lovely in her kinetic reading habits, in her soft and delicious ironies.

So I made an early deal with the voices: aural hallucinations, spooky connections, spirits in the crystal spheres. Bad wiring correctible by a cocktail of chemicals right off a shrink's pharmacology pad. We can fix you, Big Pharm says. Whatdya need? A tweak here, a pat there? Or we've got the full chem-deal that will oust that tired, old, raggedy self and that crabby anxiety and give you a brand-spanking new You. Take it for a test drive? I picture those adults from my childhood with one hand behind the back crammed with pharmaceuticals for me, to smooth me out and return me to the herd.

I thanked my genetic stars that I got a set of amusing, even soothing, voices. I knew, after a little research, that there were much worse versions: anxious, screeching, do-bad-shit voices. But mine, they seemed interested in the world and, well . . . self-contained. As if they only needed me like a hired limousine to carry them around while they had a good time hooting out the sunroof. The one I came to like best (who must have thought it was just a funny thing to do) was the one who just said my name out startlingly loud and clear. Just once, like tapping me on the shoulder and then not being there when I turn around. Very funny. Like a lot of funny, repetition was apparently the key to hilarity. And as far as I could tell, maybe they were all the same voice, just saying different things. But the clearest one, the one I didn't need to double-take on to understand, that was the one that just said, "Jake." I should have given him a name, just to tame him. But I didn't. Alas, Rex was already taken.

When you're a kid you want to be like all the other kids. So the voices got stuffed. But afterward, in my early thirties especially, I thought of the voices like owning up to a quirk that might become sort of charming in the longer run. You know, like a funny way of sneezing that everyone seems to like. Or a chuckle that always catches other people off guard and makes them laugh about your laugh. And anyway, the voices weren't going away apparently, so I thought Marnie would be a good place to try out their charms.

I still didn't tell anyone—well, just her—about the voices. The shit storm was still too clearly painful. The dodged shit storm—that's how I saw it. No voices, really, I told them in second grade. Just must have been listening to myself blither. Or is that blather? But the voices, like The Dude, abide, and abide in a kind of negotiated détente. That is, any momentous slipup and I'd be surrounded by wide-eyed solicitous people meaning well but hovering over me with a handful of pharmacology to save me from myself. Talk about your sword of Damocles hanging by one horsehair. But that's ground already covered. Just wanted to be clear.

* * *

I make my living in the world of science. I think of myself as an interpreter who listens to the palaver of the assembled group of scientists who speak Science, and then I turn to the puzzled hoard of magazine buyers, and I render the science into foundational English, maybe with a cute metaphor, a diagram, a piping of my own flute. Not so different, really, from hearing voices and reporting the results to the world. What writers do. Probably how I was attracted to the science-go-between job; I was already there. So this job is what took me to Doctor of Philosophy, Ph of D, Alfred Sewall. Call me Al. Call me Fred.

The storm, threatening all morning, broke out in a gentle rain after all those apocalyptic clouds, that cumulonimbus bluster and posturing. It hissed on the rooftop, clattered in the downspout, rattled the trees into joyful dances, and smelled of ancient and perfect geometry of God's hair.

Of course, there were voices in the rain as there are in rivers and wind, but not *my* voices.

* * *

I went, at my editor's urging, to the academic conference on biogenetics, and because of the amplification system I could understand only some from the first speaker, just patches from the second. And the third, Alfred Sewall, a short man in a frumpy gray suit, didn't even bother to speak into the microphone. He read his paper in a monotone, like a funeral oration.

The difficulty wasn't because the material was too technical for me. I had done my homework as soon as my editor sent me to cover the business end of the conference. I had been doing science reporting long enough to know my alleles from my genotypes. The reason I could understand so little of the third speaker was a combination of bad P.A. system, hall acoustics like a grade-school gym and the speaker's complete disregard for the dynamic range of the twenty-buck mike there waving over his head as he putzed through his paper. He looked like he was ready to flee or fade away below the podium.

I had a sensitive little tape recorder that I could turn up to get the gist of what the guy said, so I just flipped it on and let it do the listening while I played games with the fragments quacking out over the speaker system—weird analogs to my own voices and their diffident comings and goings.

I got "intelligent strings," and that turned into cat's cradle in my idling mind. Then I heard (I think) "low-volt engine" and "crude encryption." I went with the crude in crude encryption and my notes wandered off into sexy anime and then visions of the girl with one eye and the tank top in "Futurama." Every time I write, I get the ADHD collywobbles in which I consider all sides of all words and fly off to what I began to call association picnics. Bingo, bango, bongo. And I'm off. Only the last D, the disorder part, I've never acknowledged. I don't know how other writers do it, but attention deficit is actually how I write: this brings up that, these words uncover those until I'm in the word stream and getting shit done. All stories are connected by roots; they tangle into each other like Darwin's metaphor of the tangled bank of nature in which all things are part of each other. Stories to me are made by simply lopping off one part from all the others, the great continuum where all tales reside, and giving it a title. And, yes, I also see the pitfalls in that. When the whole brain-babbling runs together with getting along every day, it is important to check the faces around you for puzzled looks. And then make corrections back toward some kind of negotiable reality. Say, "Hi there. How are the kids?" Check for small cracks in life and repair them early.

That should be written on a T-shirt somewhere.

So the gray little guy, Professor Alfred Sewall, mumbles on while I play, and the audience begins to wander off to pee (I suppose) and even start conversations with the people next to them. I guess nobody can really hear, and Dr. S doesn't seem interested in getting the mic near his face. Mercifully, he brings it to an end after about twenty minutes, there's polite applause, and a general fiddling with papers as always happens at these events. I have written down the fragments of what I heard, drawn a pretty good version of the girl with one eye and made a grocery list in my notebook. Dr. S, Dr. Seuss. I have a fair rendering of a Lorax drawn peering at fragments: "super points," "compression technology," "a biological brewery" and "social engineering." Turned out these smatterings would assemble themselves very soon like sentences trying on suits of different grammars.

Dr. S is gone immediately. That evening I do my recording-device magic and reconstitute the doctor's speech and make plans to find him in the morning as soon as I can to ask him questions. He said, essentially, that he could, *someone* could, break down an animal into its component chemistry and register that recipe into zeroes and ones and then compress the whole set of instructions into storage and then later bring out (hash functions) the recipe and reassemble the critter. Cold storage? Cryogenics? Please! All we'd have to do is take someone apart, record the particulars of his or her unique set of algorithms and then wait until we wanted it back together again. Number ghosts. Songs in the wires.

Talk about warm storage. Here's the disk with grandma and the flash drive with grandpa. We'll put them together for the weekend and a have a picnic, just like the old days. And there I went. Taking off. My editor would bring it back to earth; that's why they got the big bucks. Gonzo journalism hadn't made it into science reporting just yet, but there was room.

The next day I searched the conference high and low to find

Dr. Sewall and couldn't raise hide nor hair, spit nor image. Cold trail. So I went back to the conference publication and found out he taught and worked at the agriculture university across town. Maybe he was talking about cattle herds or goose flocks or sheep. But my recording had the *he* pronoun, once in a while a *she*. I'm sure he was talking about people. He groused about not having the funding to try out any but the most basic amino-acid conversion. He said, he mumbled, that he could do it. But the scale for larger conversions would take lots of National Science Foundation dough. And then something about Dr. Frankenstein having his own money to work with. Pause for a laugh that never came.

I got what would be useful from the conference: epigenetics, so-called blank genes, and even CSI stuff (the most well attended speakers). The Dr. S material didn't seem to fit anywhere. It was computer science slash cell biology slash bio-chem slash genetics and then a few more AI slashes. No wonder he couldn't get funding. That place for the short description at the top of the application form—what the hell would he put there? How about: I want to make virtual people? Gimme money. Or even better: How to get mom and dad out of the nursing home and onto a hard drive.

How much fun was this going to be! I'd write the outline of the contracted article and then go see Dr. S on my own. I had no idea what that would lead to, but I did know that the expenses would be tax deductible.

* * *

I went home, and Marnie was there, my crime-fighting partner. She was legs-up on the couch in an old sweatshirt—our preferred crime-fighting costumes—and after the usual Kato-Green Hornet banter, I told her about Dr. Sewall. The whole crime-fighting joke started so long ago neither of us remembers the beginning. It just seemed infinitely extendable and useful for everything from sex to domestic disputes. So we kept it. I told her that Dr. S was a mad scientist who I had to pursue to the ends of his Ag-lair, bring him back alive, debrief him even if he wore boxers. That sort of stuff. She was an artist and prone to bouts of seriousness. While I, I Jake James—two first names, no baggage please but a set of eternal voices occupying my head—I found high seriousness nearly incomprehensible and certainly unsustainable for any length of time. She once called me the Labrador puppy of attention deficit. I took it as a compliment and claimed many butts sniffed.

* * *

The rain and wind had slivered the air. The first load of fall leaves had taken over the sidewalks outside our apartment and adhered like decoupage. There was that wonderful disorder between seasons when weather sloughs back and forth as if inviting applause for its outrageous special effects. There was a char on the air and no insects. I would sometimes find Marnie watching out the window like a cat, and then she would point out the colors and hues just like my voices did.

I'm going to tell the next part out of order, so get ready.

The first conversation I had with Dr. S went like this.

Dr. S, apparently in mid-rant already, ". . . that's why the English have such bad teeth. Their mothers gorge on sugar through the rainy winters and compromise the baby's dental arch. The sugar binges narrow the dental arch in utero and their teeth don't fit. Worse yet, the narrow dental arch is almost impossible to fit with decent false teeth or bridges. So the whole damn country's full of bad teeth because of self-indulgence during pregnancy. Let's not even get started on the German delight in discovering thalidomide to get rid of nausea during pregnancy. And it worked! No nausea—just babies with flippers. You know, it's not even like this is secret information—what you put in your body gets into the baby. Full stop. Put in food and water. Another stop. Lots of chemicals and a couple of glasses of wine? That's what I call a scientific experiment on a fetus. And it's amazing how many are willing participants in that shitty science. Blame? Fuck that. The word 'stupidity' excludes the word blame. No blame. Just stupid."

Me: "So your experiments have shown that . . ."

Dr. S: "My experiments? *My* experiments? I'm just trying to round up the information into packages that can be stored. That's it. Very modest. And, alas, that's why the NSF doesn't give a shit about my work."

Me: "But at the conference . . ."

Dr. S: "Oh the conference? So you were there when my esteemed colleagues realized the valuable consequences of my work. How my work could further their work. How . . . what to say about my colleagues? A little story: the algorithm that made Google founders billionaires was originally designed to seek out names on the web, to find academics whose names were referenced in their colleagues' work, so that the number of times referenced could be submitted to a university committee for retention, tenure and promotion to full professor. It is a cunning algorithm. It's a capitalist's wet dream is what it is. And that is the business of science in America today—capitalism. Promotion and tenure everywhere."

I let him talk because I had no other choice. His gray hair began a dance early on, a tango I think. Then with the Google business he began to nod and there was something like a waltz occurring on his head . . . two three. He used his glasses in his hand like a series of punctuation marks. The combined effect was kinetic and riveting, and more than a little unnerving as if his eyes might get cartoon-spirals and his ears begin to spin and emit smoke. From dental arches to Google to capitalism, I hung on for the ride to see where we'd end up. The doctor conducting a workshop in can-you-follow-me? This was a different guy from the one I watched mumble at the conference.

Dr. S: ". . . the garden, you see, becomes a physical manifestation of the gardener after a time: a simulacrum in which thought and habit is made manifest by the growing plants." He seemed to be lecturing somewhere over my shoulder. "So the shaping takes place out of the information available to shape. The early errors of a gardener are more important than the later errors. The dental arch is relatively late. A bad brain relatively early. But here's the key: the entire arrangement is one of contingencies, and with good information, you get good conformation. Take a tree. A blue spruce with all the right air, sun, water, nutrients and space will grow true in color and, most important, conformation. It will be shaped ideally: to capture more light, to reproduce, etc. The space and air and sun are early information too. Very important. Any lacking there and the entire project of growth is at risk."

It didn't seem to bother him that I had put down my paper and pen. It only seemed to matter that I was listening, looking at him talk. And I was getting the idea better by just listening than by trying to write it down. He wafted back and forth between the fucks and shits and words like "genetic contingencies." I found the wafting to be great comfort and in sync with my own juggling mind.

Here's how the whole conversation got started.

I had asked a secretary in the first building I came to where I might find Dr. Sewall. She didn't recognize the name but looked him up for me, gave me a campus map and circled the Ag complex. Always be nice to secretaries; my mantra: they know everything and can make things easy or difficult for you.

I found the Ag complex at his university by asking the first student I saw wearing a flannel shirt in the light rain. The animal barns were on the edge of campus, so the prevailing winds carried the manure smell off toward the experimental forest. The barns reminded me of state fairs and my grandfather's horse barn. From out of the rain into the barn, wet into dry, light into dark, I stood letting my eyes get used to the gloom punctuated by a few hanging lights. A student was sleeping on two hay bales. I walked by the row of cows where each animal had a decoration of plastic ear tags as if decked out for a parade—yellow, orange, red, blue. I could hear poultry but not see any. I tried to look like I knew where I was going, figuring somebody here would stop me and ask my business. But nobody did. I waved at one student and he waved back, so I kept touring. I was wandering a complicated barn that was full up with Noah's own bestiary and the voices of the Ark babbled all around. Dr. S apparently had experimental digs out in the zoo section of the university where I expected Charlotte's web hanging from the next rafter with a message on it for me.

The stalls were truncated by cross-corridors. Air seemed to be kept moving by some hidden fans, and the walk became pleasant and surreal. The light and smell and steady thump of my shoes on the concrete floor was like a soundtrack. Now there were horses. Then sheep, noisier but like altos singing with the growing sopranos of the poultry. I knew I was getting closer to poultry by the acrid tinge to the air. I turned another corridor, and there was a string of doors, people doors, I figured. They could be offices or labs. One had a light on so I knocked. A grad student told me he thought Dr. S had digs in the next building, and I should just wend that way until I couldn't hear the sheep anymore and that would be about where he was. Dr. S was not really considered an Ag guy, anyway. The student didn't know what he even did, but said he came around the Ag building wearing a suit, so everyone knew who he was, that he didn't really belong. And then, the student gave a quick assessment of the value of wearing ties in an agricultural setting: catching it in a threshing machine, having an animal go for it. He told me most of the critters around us here bite. I don't think he had talked to anyone for a while, so he and his voice babbled on like my voices but with less passion: "They don't all the time, but every damn one of them do, once in a while, bite." He went on. "You'd think chickens would be exempt, but they're not. Don't even get me started on ducks. I went into this looking for something that didn't bite, or most rarely. You'd think there was something, wouldn't you? Domesticated animals. Domesticated! But no. Every damn one of them wants a piece of you. I saw a cow eat a guy's Nikon once. Just grabbed it and bit the lens off and spit it out. Thought it might be something to eat. That's how they all operate. Something to eat, something to bite. Oh, yeah. And then something to fuck. I don't know why I keep doing this—oh yeah, I do, a job. My mother wanted me to play the piano, but would I practice . . . ?" I thought he seemed, as I often did, to be listening to some rambling discourse in his brain and letting part of it run out his mouth. I pondered giving him the high-five of the brotherhood of voices but decided no and backed away. Clearly, his voices had backed up and were waiting for an audience. He hadn't learned to talk to the animals, I guessed.

I thanked him and scurried away from the sound of sheep. Eventually I found the office of Dr. Sewall tucked into a complicated set of rooms and locked doors as if someone had concocted a video game of doors. Get around the locked ones and see what's in the unlocked ones. I found one marked *Dr. Sewall* and knocked. Silence. I tried the door thinking I might enter an anteroom or find a secretary. But I found the lair of Dr. S, just as I would in a monster movie. But no Dr. S.

The lab was small but intensely crowded. A bank of computers, some kind of oscilloscopes, a stack of centrifuges, what looked like an empty kennel, and, in the corner, a warm orange glow from a sealed acrylic box with small, silvery ducts leading in and out of it. There was a barely perceptible hum. Maybe a low D. There were no other lights on, but I could see well enough by the bluish light of a high window, and the lab looked to be densely efficient. Efficient at what? I got closer to the box.

In one corner was a dark gray-brown mass. I thought it looked like a plant of some kind, but it had no vertical structure. It was a lump. But I thought I saw the lump move. The light was so weird that I distrusted what I thought I saw. I waited. It didn't move again, at least not like the first time. I got the feeling I was in a place I had no business, but the door had been open. I thought I better call out, see if anyone was around. Maybe a grad student, maybe a shepherd. I called out, and from what seemed far away, a voice answered, a dry high voice. I called again. Again the answer—just "over here." So, of course, voice-ready all my life, I went back to the blob in the glow to see if I was talking to it.

When I was twelve and began to have solid opinions about the world, my voices solidified too, as if they somehow became more substantial and hardened by hormones. So conversing here with a bowl of oatmeal, though not my everyday experience, was easily within the realm of possibility. I had been prepared for the "other" all my life. Like St. Francis for the wildlife. Like Ahab for the taste of saltwater. At age twelve, hormones and voices produced a concert unmatched in the rest of my short life. I remember I couldn't wait to wake up and listen to the world both in and out of my head. Sometimes I wanted to jump straight up and never come down.

I had seen all the blob movies from the actual, *The Blob*, on to all the viscous liquid-like moving things that ate the world. I was ready to parley with this one. My only regret was that Marnie wouldn't be here at the moment of contact. "Over in 201." So, okay, that's not going to be a blob talking. I retraced my steps and found 201 and the small dry voice—another grad student who also, it seemed, hadn't talked to anyone in days. I had come into a desert of sorts where humans were spaced out among the animals and rolled tumbleweeds of hay.

I told him who I was looking for. He waited. So I told him why. "Oh, he'd be glad to tell you about what he's doing. None of the rest of us think it's worth listening to. But a reporter—sure. Most of the rest of us are Ag people with a smattering of bird and fish people. You can tell them by their hats for some reason. The bird people always wear . . ."

I thanked him, got directions to where I might find Dr. S and worked my way out of the maze. He had a regular office but wasn't there. A note on the door said he was in the cafeteria if anyone wanted to find him.

Then, in the cafeteria, we had that first conversation, or what I came to think of as the listening. I didn't mention that I'd been to his lab uninvited. He seemed the standard amount of crabby I expected from the conference, but not the wide-ranging crabby, the omni-crabby, of a dissolute philosopher—English women and dental arches, Google, etc. I wanted to ask him about the gray-brown thing that moved, but I didn't. I asked him if I could see his lab sometime. He said no. There was nothing there I'd be interested in. I said let me be the judge of that, and he said no and got up, went to his office and that was that. Or would have been that.

I drove back home preparing my tale for Marnie—the lights, the sounds, the weird denizens of the Ag complex, the blob, the animal voices, the movement. The movement. It moved, shifted really. Or it didn't. Perfect tautology.

It all—Ag building, grad students, sheep sounds—got me to thinking how I'd write the article. It could be about masks, the ones we wear, the ones the world wears, and how interesting it is to pull back an edge and start to peek under. What delicious surprises there are. Also what devastating surprises there are. Still, we must peek, and peek we do. I'd write about the peeking.

Chapter II

Marnie was burbling full of Modernism. She was preparing a speech, or an introduction rather, to an art opening at her gallery. The main attraction was part of the collection of a local businessman—nether Modernists plus lesser pieces by more famous Modernists. The gist of her speech was that the Modernists had tried to revolutionize the art world at the beginning of the 20th century by introducing more information into art: not new, but more. Paintings, instead of the regular colors would be alternative colors (Fauvists), or instead of regular perspective consistent with a real world would be the fusion of several different perspectives from different times and angles (Cubists). But the Modernist movement(s) with all its beginnings was really just a disenchantment with what they thought was art's poor sampling of reality. They asked: When we looked at the world, didn't we also fuse our memories and desires along with what our senses picked up from the canvas or sculpture? Didn't we, in the act of seeing art, bring different times and places and colors and even imaginative interpretations to the very act of looking? Shouldn't art keep up with this human multi-tasking? She went on like this, but all I heard was Dr. S (who, by this time, I had thoroughly rendered as Dr. Seuss in my brain—"This one has a little car, this one has a little star. Oh, what a lot of things there are."). Dr. S ranting, Dr. S keeping his critter secret until he could blow away the world. Marnie said Juan Gris was the most underrated of them all because he died young; Picasso the most highly rated because he died very old. But it was Gris, Picasso's countryman, who cracked open the old mold of the shopworn literal: haystacks in the sunlight, the hazy impression of a rainy street scene. Gris made *the jump,* and I kept thinking that Dr. S was making the jump, if I understood him right. Modernism was the movement that opened the door to, for example, abstract impressionism and the paintings that claimed a higher and realer expression of human emotions in paint. Jackson Pollock and Kandinsky and Tobey and Ernst—they cracked the code in the second phase. Dr. S was really saying that the next level of information is now available, like Juan Gris did. The door's open. Did that thing really move in his lab? So what? Was it new information or old information just reconstituted?

I began the swirl back and forth between Marnie's Modernism—a new real—and Dr. S's theoretical claims that life was just a package of information and was infinitely extendable. Maybe my voices were just the aural equivalence of the Modernist painter's vision. Maybe it was the same gift. Maybe, like them, I should develop a manifesto so I could tell the world about my vision, my additions to puny, everyday consciousness? Talk about inviting medication! I would just be asking for the "there-there," the "how do you feel about . . ." the condescending arm rub of comfort. I guess all that stuff stuck in my craw more than I realized. I listened to Marnie try out her Modernism spiel on me. As a listener—maybe it's the voices and their sometimes running commentary—I'm likely to latch onto a piece of information and run off with it, over there behind the shrubs where I can gnaw on it a little, make goo-goo eyes at it, interrogate it more closely. Not ideal, I know. I needed to focus and follow, focus and follow.

So, hang on a second. I want to add in here another conversation, kind of a hearing-of-voices, but out loud in the regular way of talking to someone. I read that there was a huge starfish die-off in the Pacific Ocean off the coast of Washington. I was drinking beer with a friend, and I offered that, of course, aliens had come down to take the starfish's ability to reproduce its limbs. I had heard the whip-tailed lizard and other critters could do the same thing, and we should be aware in case the lizards were next. I figured (okay, *three* beers later) that humans would be taken last because we couldn't do what even the lowly plant could do—reproduce ourselves out of a fragment. So the starfish die-off—had to be aliens . . . "Oh, but seriously, why can't we make new parts?" And he says, "Well, theoretically, we can. We can make them . . . but the real problem is installation, I guess." Turns out some kind of petri-dish cookery will make lots of human parts but something is missing. Doctors can't make them stay. My bad knee needs a new meniscus. So they grow me one and when they try to install it, the new part wanders off. It doesn't know where to stay or what to do. Not enough information got transferred in growing the new part? And then the royal scientific "we," he says, "We don't know why it won't work. We can't address it. Probably some proteins missing, amino acid blocks. Who knows?" I think that my voices would know; they just wouldn't tell me. Damn their ethereal hides! Why can't they just give me the word, solve this world for me? I never wanted anything from them but entertainment when I was a kid. But now I want meaning. Isn't that the shits! Same voices: it's me who wants something different. It's my rising longing after the world that screws up the sweet relationship we had when I was a kid.

So I suggest that I know a guy who . . .

Let me start again. I know a guy who thinks that the only problem in this whole business of replacement parts is just better information. And that's exactly what my beer-drinking science-friend thinks too. But Dr. S is—theoretically again—cooking up the gray blob that might get the job done. So welcome to my world where my lady friend and my Dr. S connive like actors in a play to assemble something compelling. Chekov's gun in the first act is required to go off by the fifth act. I want, I want and the voices demur. I wait patiently for them to prove useful. Why else are they wired in my head in the on position? In the wild, would they warn me about the beast stalking me and save me and themselves?

I have to get back to Dr. S. He doesn't write; he doesn't call. Though I've courted him like a lover, he rejects my suit. So instead, I finish listening to Marnie's Modernism talk and applaud.

I say, "Socks will be knocked off. There will be socks ten deep across the floor."

She says, "I'm supposed to deliver this while partway up a ladder. The director wants me doing something the Modernists would approve of, and he came up with the ladder in lieu of my refusal to do it naked. Did you ever climb a ladder in high heels?"

"Stepladder?"

"I think so, but . . ."

"Okay, so here's my ladder-wise advice. Go up only far enough so you can rest your notes or even your elbows on the top. You can put a glass of water on the little shelf that sticks out—be sure that's all the way out; it's what makes the ladder stable. And so that is the entire store of my ladder information. You're on your own for the rest. Why not naked?"

"Only for you I do naked speeches." She turned away, that way she has, that turning-away thing she does that makes me go jelly inside and smile. And I'm pretty sure she knows it too.

We make love without chasing around. We make love, and it occurs to me, though just fleetingly, that making love is just the right information at the right time. The whole human critter is set up for sex to be the right information at exactly the right time. Even done badly.

Marnie's introduction is a fine success, ladder and all. She's up there in her high heels using the top as a podium. A minor Max Ernst is just behind her head: some plant or leaf drawing with typing on it. I can't get over the way this information thing is stuck in my head, how it now colors everything I see and do. It joins the mask business. The whole notion of the tyranny of binary. Yeah, Pythagoras. Why haven't the whole numbers of zeroes and ones been split—like fractions? My computer friends explain that zero and one are really just off and on, or even more really just a micro-voltage difference between what designates the zero and the one. Sure, but all that mush between? Isn't that what Dr. S is proposing that all the mush between is chockful of information we need? Isn't that why a homegrown meniscus won't stay? Is there a dent in my DNA that turned on the voices and their iterations and cosmic echoes? A crappy shred of protein that hooks up "wrong?" Why didn't I get the vision of an eagle instead? The whole subject of superpowers occurs to me. As it should. Was Modernism really just a 20th century awakening to let in alternative realities? I should have listened closer to Marnie's intro. It would have prepared me for the alternatives I was about to bang into headfirst.

Max Ernst was doing just that, Marnie informs me back at home, after hearing my new obsession. He was fascinated by the irrational, the Freudian sub- and pre- and un-consciousnesses. He painted out of his refugee status—refugee from his father's art, from war, from consciousness, from the fraudulent surfaces of what he thought were passing for reality in Europe.

So now I had Max and Albert, Ernst and Sewall. This thing going around and around in my head. I knew the way to get it out was write it out. I had to talk to Dr. S again, but it seemed the only way to do that was to go to the university and stalk him.

Chapter III

I thought that the way in with Dr. S would be to study his world, but it turned out he was in his own world all right, but a world largely inaccessible to others. No one else in science seemed to be doing what he was doing, for one thing. And the second thing was that he is such a . . . what? I want to say "crabby fuck," but that's a gloss on what he is. Maybe he's a cartoon crabby fuck with curmudgeon tendencies and misanthrope moons rising to his conflicted disdain for all human activity. Oh, Jesus, Mary and Joseph. See. That's still only part of it. I have to add that he seemed to be in pain in at least one of his undiagnosed organelles. In the old *Li'l Abner* cartoons, a character was described as "his goodness glands was squoze." Something like that maybe. A distress that wouldn't go away.

Yet, I pictured him there in his lab tending like a kindly farmer to some gray-brown thing in a bluish-orange light.

I went to his lab again and peeked in at the thing, the blob. It seemed to be resting comfortably. I thought: *Hi, thing. I get the feeling you and I are going to get to know each other sometime in the future. Whither goest thou?* I thought maybe it was biblical or going to be biblical and might speak King James. Prophetic, apocalyptic—there would be smiting, of course. But there was no action in the Lucite corner, so I went to plan B: attend Dr. S's classes. I hit up my newfound secretary contact for a schedule of his classes and sat in.

As I walked toward his class building, it seemed the university paths floated with all the possibilities in the world. Besides the few cellphone dropouts from reality pasted to their tiny screens and walking the zombie walk, most students chatted at each other with a young-adult frenzy fueled by hormones and pheromones and sweet-smelling soaps and caffeine. They seemed to tick with possibilities: of mating, of rearranging the dreary evil-smelling reality of their parents into the world of logical-positive idealism of their classes. They cooked in their own joy and angst. All possible worlds were possible. I could almost hear their hundreds of voices rattling as I walked with them. But I had my own voices and didn't need or want theirs. The morning sun coated us all, sinner and sinned against, voiced and voicelessly blessed without prejudice. One of my voices pointed out that patina of gold momentarily outlining the Fine Arts building's Italianate façade. I know, I say. I know; I see it already.

I was writing, of course. I always wrote when I walked with strangers as if I were receiving their energy like sunlight on my shoulders. I delighted in the tiny cracks that appeared in the dull surface of the world, cracks that let in other possibilities, especially the possibility of the whole sham of surfaces falling away with ceremonial clamor and trumpets—peeking under the masks. The shams didn't fall. But I felt ready anyway, more prepared for the great sloughing into truth than anyone.

I entered the big lecture room just in time to hear Dr. S extolling the virtues of the mechanisms—there are many, it turns out—that kill us.

". . . they make room. For more. For more of us, more cells, more and different everything. The key fact is that there are a number of built-in failures in living tissue. I'm not just talking about the errors that produce cancers or birth defects or hereditary disease. That's all very interesting and a topic for another day. What I'm referring to is the tendency of cells or collections of cells to fail. I like to think of them as collaborations of cells and one of the failures is at the level of that collaboration. Imagine a meeting that begins with great civility and pomp and even ritual. But pretty soon one of the participants fires a rubber band across the table at the person across from him. Then, in time, someone else starts chucking pencils at the ceiling to see if he can make one stick, but the pencils start to rain down on the proceedings. And then . . . well, you can see where this is going. Pretty soon—the edge of chaos. Then chaos itself. The meeting's over."

Dr. S was apparently in fine fettle, sawing the air like a Shakespearean ham. Ernest. He was Alfred—but he was also earnest, and the students were getting it. This was his element, unlike the academic conference. He seemed to have the script for this gig—the pauses, the eye rollings, the little dance as he spun toward the board. He used the light switches to portray the off and on signals of the cell mechanisms; he lobbed a small piece of chalk at the sleeper in the first row. He continued.

"Well, the cells are loaded with delinquent possibilities. The *design* of the cells is fraught with the potential for error. And it's more than just the old maxim about complexity inviting error. No. The design itself is like a cosmic joke of sorts. A joke about death and failure and cellular incompetence. Or, put in a more hopeful context, the design invites re-design. By peering into cellular shenanigans, we are challenged to make the whole business better. The design-to-fail says to the scientist: 'Bet you can't make a better one. Go ahead. I dare you. Go ahead. You think you're so smart? If you fix this, it'll break that. See? Don't screw with the amino acids! I'm warning you. Go ahead and clone, and you'll find some key ingredient missing.' Remember the sheep named Dolly?"

Did Rex just get a pedigree, I wondered? Was the doctor laying out his recipe for gray oatmeal? I pictured the orange glow of Rex's Lucite lair, pictured him rearing up on hind . . . okay, so pseudopods, and then squirting out the breathing holes and declaring himself free. I was off.

And he was off. This lecture was completely different from the conference fiasco; this had sound and fury. I sat smiling at this master-of-the-mind-getting-off-on-itself. Dr. S was just like me and my ADHD but in an awful suit with an awful tie and a stick up his butt. He paced as he spoke, came to the end of some invisible tether, spun around and paced back. The pacing had a touch of Groucho Marx to it. I again thought of the blob of oatmeal, amino acids sulking in the Lucite corner of his cage. Maybe that was the solution to the design-to-fail Dr. S was describing. Had the doctor eliminated the fail? Even if it just sat there and didn't fail, that would certainly be something better than the proverbially sliced bread.

"That sheep was only partial. What was missing? We'll get to the particulars of that later, but for now: what was missing was the elegance of what I call the 'failure system.' It's the way the system fails that is the key to its vitality at the cellular level. Do we have to put up with death? No. Not really. We can accept the challenge to re-design the thing. But that will be the subject of a four hundred level course and this is a two hundred level.

"So one last thing. A scientist asks what is the mechanism of cell failure, and as I said, it turns out there are many. The cosmic joke of death. Yes. But also in the long run—the very long sine-wave if you will—there is a general culling of the old in favor of the new: cell, individual, species, genus, etc. Nature favors the newest version in general. So that challenge—to make it new—is really inherent already in the system. You can fiddle with the particulars but be sure to honor the general." The newest version? The blob in the cage?

He paced. He pulled on an ear lobe. He put his hands together in front of him making a church—here's the church, here's the steeple, open the door and see all the people? I pictured his lab in the hay bales, Rex boxed in glow; was this cell lecture working itself out into some kind of pabulum of immortality?

"Mitochondria, for instance, was once a free-range critter that for some fortuitous reason found a home in the human replication system. Now it goes to work schlepping materials to the nucleus, never stopping for lunch. But also added its own error-prone system to the already error-ridden business of reproduction. Be sure to feed your mitochondria—keep them happy—so that the rest of the system can get reproducing.

"For Tuesday: memorize the terms on the handout sheet. They're basic to where we go next with this stuff. Come prepared.

"Oh, and how do you tell a male chromosome from a female chromosome? That's right. Pull their genes down." The laughter that was missing from the conference joke.

I waited for the auditorium to clear to catch him on his way back to his office. But he disappeared out a door in the front of the room before I could get down to him. I went around outside the building and saw him booking it across the campus toward the Ag buildings.

I scurried through the cows and their calm farting, the sheep and their baleful eyes peering out of the dark pens, the heavy breathing of pigs. Somehow Dr. S got into his lab well ahead of me and was already busy as if he had transported himself directly or knew of some back way under the maze of animals.

"What?" he asked when I knocked on the open door. "Oh. You again."

"I wanted to talk to you if you have time. About your work. Your ideas."

"I don't have ideas. I have work. I'm a builder."

But I could see he was still on a roll from class and wouldn't mind, I thought, talking a little more about what he did. "So what exactly do you build?" I glanced at the blob in the back of the lab. He followed my glance.

"So you've met Rex? I don't lock the door. I probably should. So let's say you've met Rex."

"Not really. Though I guess I've what? Maybe, peered at him. And wondered. Why a *him*?"

"He's actually nothing and everything. I just liked the idea of Rex, you know. Like Oedipus Rex or Rex a dog, a king of things in general. But ironically, of course. More like Oedipus than Rin-Tin-Tin."

I kept looking at Dr. S for signs. Where was he coming from? Talking to him was like talking to someone on the phone: the facial clues were not there. Or maybe, the opposite, there were too many clues: eye twinkles, look-aways, sniffs and snorts, head-scratchings with his middle finger. That sort of stuff.

Marnie and I had a whole middle-finger system. "Sure I'd like to go shopping for art supplies"—middle finger scratch—"Sure, we can double date with them; they seem like nice people"—finger-gun to head: two shots, middle-finger scratch. I was sure Dr. S and his Lorax named Rex were in on the game.

"So, Rex? Does he do any tricks?" Interviewing brilliance, I thought. Where could we go from here?

"Yes, tricks. So far just one good one. He seems to leave some gray powder there in the corner of his cage sometimes. Like I'm supposed to clean up after him. I always think of this residue as broken zeroes and ones, you know. Part of a circle, a half a line. But very small, of course. Since Rex is really a series of computer commands, what could he poop out? Maybe ions. Maybe his cellular mistakes. That's what I hope, of course. That he's fixing himself, repairing . . . Who knows? It looked like gray dust, even under a microscope. Oh, a little like spores too. That was spooky."

Dr. S paced back to where Rex huddled in his corner. Huddled? He had me thinking that way, now. Then the doctor pulled out his shirttail and waved it at Rex. Really? I thought.

Dr. S said, "I always like to let him know that I'm his friend—not that whole Geppetto mistake. That I-made-you-so-listen-up. That mistake. I'm just saying hi. Do you need anything? How's it going?" He flapped his shirttail again. Rex remained silent and in his corner. Was Dr. S giving me the complete goof trip? He continued: "The only interesting thing I've done here is get the basic set of instructions partly right. I have no illusions about getting very many instructions right, just a few basic ones. Dr. Frankenstein shouting, 'It's alive!' Nothing like that. But I think in some really fundamental way, it *is* alive." The doctor peered into the blob. "Good boy, Rex," he said. "Good boy."

And so he sat down and gave me all the caveats. There was no spinal cord, the nerves were rudimentary (more like a cartoon version of real nerves, he added) and, alas, no mitochondrial reproduction. Then the poet in him came out, the great quotes for my article: "No Yin to its Yang, no Cheech to its Chong." That was the best. Also: moon/sun, shimmy/shammy and boku/maru (I looked it up later; it's a Kurt Vonnegut reference).

The doctor kicked back in his chair, feet on his desk. "And that's that. I mean I couldn't get the time of day with this at the conference. Colleagues? Did you stay long enough to hear the crap they *were* interested in?" This in stentorian tones, announcer style. "'Folding and protein transcription in RNA copying.' Yep, I said to myself. It sure does. Yup. Nobody is doing anything like Rex." He glanced over at Rex. "I'll tell you who is though. Sci-fi magazines, that's who. The most interesting genetics is being done in sci-fi mags, not in laboratories."

I madly scribbled, reached into my pocket to turn on my recorder, went from pencil to pen. I thought, Good boy, Rex. Good boy.

I left Dr. S with my article percolating in my brain. I always percolated before imposing any order on the thing. The order would come out of the percolating action, I think. All the way back in the car I wrote in my head.

Marnie had left me a text. In the time it took me to drive home, a news item caught her eye: it was about the EPA investigating some guy's claim that his house had been invaded by some kind of slime that he had tried to kill with bleach and then the whole thing changed to gray dust and went everywhere in his house. He was a vacuum cleaner salesman—that was the part that was newsworthy. Vacuum cleaner salesman overcome by dust. Dust one, vacuum industry zero.

I drove along, took the slow way home, wrote the story in my head—listened for it and made it into a story.

I sell vacuums for a living. Not door to door in the cartoon salesman sense. I am the manager of a substantial sales force. I have experience, expertise. I know suction. I know amps. And cubic feet per second, good plastic from bad plastic. I consider myself a reasonable person, but I have to say that the irony was not lost on me—I sell vacuums and I am assaulted by dust. What the hell am I supposed to do with that? I am a person of regular habits and an adequate imaginary life. I respect the Easter Bunny, Tooth Fairy, Santa Claus as cultural requirements for a sound childhood. To science fiction I prefer engineering. A vacuum cleaner is, looked at properly, the tool that has allowed us to live inside in healthy conditions. The vacuum is responsible for civilization in key ways. And then came the dust.

I was going to turn on the car radio but stopped and let the story fructify itself out the windshield. But I did hum along with the story as the words came tumbling to me.

It had always been there.

I think now that it was like stacking boxes in order to get at something up high. The first box alone won't get you far enough. But a couple more and there you are. There *they* are. The pieces had always been near each other but it took a flood—a minor flood at that—and the perfect temporary disorder swirling brown water can cause. Then the rearrangement happened, probably always would have happened. There was nothing to be done about it, either. The ingredients were patient. Only we are impatient in the world, rushing around to get things temporarily done. While there and there, and over there again are all those parts just waiting to come together.

That's how it happened. The water joined what was lying around in the landscape. Again: vacuums, dust, water—I get it, I get it.

I was sure Darwin had written something on the subject, and I went about digging through his works looking to see if he had anticipated this assembling business. I thought since he noticed that Nature continually altered its various critters out of constant necessity, out of the demand of life to survive, that he certainly would have written about all the potential forms of life just lying around in constituent pieces waiting on the universe's shelf. And then . . . I think a big wind might also have worked as well as water. Or something biblical—a whirlwind, a burning bush, the lion's den. But the flood was nothing more than Johnson Creek rising as it always had in the spring, rising through the grasses, then up to the tree line and then through the rip-rap we'd installed to keep the bank, and finally, as it did every ten years or so, up to the back porch. No farther. Not in my memory. The back porch was memory's high water.

I edited out a bunch of other Darwin stuff here. It was just getting in the way. I meandered. Like a river. Like the babbling in the river, the babbling voices that every river has. You don't even have to listen very closely. There's just this talking and talking and talking going on.

My son first pointed it out. He thought it was some kind of growth. We looked up "slime mold" together to see if that's what it was. Turns out that slime mold can be either a plant or an animal depending on the amount of food available to it. At the cellular level it will be single-celled in times of abundance, and then in times of famine, the cells will aggregate and go in search of food. We talked about how convenient this would be, how much fun to "go plant" for a while on the couch with a giant bag of potato chips. Then combine cells and wander off to find new bags—FunYuns maybe.

Since the blob occurred right where the water had come to, we thought maybe the flood had brought it food. The next day it was bigger and the day after that we thought maybe we should try a little bleach on it before it got into the beams under the porch. Apparently, as I see now, it had waited since the Big Bang for someone to pour bleach on it, waited with open interstices in its DNA. So sodium hypochlorite, bleach, it seems was the salt necessary to make the thing—the box stacked on top that allowed the thing to finally reach out to time. And be.

In general, I consider myself sympathetic to all forms of life—smelly ones, icky ones, stinging ones, ugly ones, even vicious ones. We're all in this together. We all want to succeed in our own way. Leave me alone, I'll leave you alone. But that doesn't seem to be the plan. The leaving alone part. Alas.

Darwin again; we compete. Even when we're not immediately competing, it seems, something in us knows that we will eventually need the same food as everything else around us. So sooner or later we take on the fight for that food. It knew at some level. I knew, probably at the same level.

This gaseous stuff I'd have to fix later if I wrote this down to keep. The edge of town, really the long way home, but I was getting interested in seeing how the story turned out. I kept going away from home to get the thing out and written in my head.

So it was no more an alien than I was. Both of us were just a matter of the required assembly, and the only thing heroic about the whole business was that we coincided in time. I think many heroes go out to slay dragons. Only a few of us actually find a dragon to slay or be slain by. It took a while, but eventually I realized how lucky I was to find one.

Dragon? Back to the action. Red barns, the smell of manure, a patch of premature daffodils along a fence row—dragon slaying. Regular stuff where there are dragons.

My son and I thought we had kept it out of the house with the bleach and were going to bury the rest of it and hope it made good fertilizer. But as I said, the bleach completed it, and it no longer looked the same. The blob that appeared as slime mold *did* disappear—job done. But the new thing was not a blob anymore. It was hungry. Wouldn't you be if you had waited for all of time? To be or not to be? What a stupid question, Hamlet. To *be* of course. How *long* to be, now there's a different question, and that's the real question regarding suicide.

My son filled a jar with the old goo because he wanted to take it to school. The old stuff was really just the snakeskin sloughed off, but the "snake" was still in there. It took less than a week to realize we had failed with the bleach and the thing had indeed made its way into the house. Everywhere in the house.

This time it looked like a fine white dust nearly indistinguishable from our regular dust. But the while dust was uniform in size, smaller than regular dust that would clump up when scraped together, and if you looked closely you could see that moving some of dust also moved other dust without touching it. There was a sympathy, somehow, between any part of the dust and the rest of the dust. Still we lived with it at first until it began to move things in the house: lamps on tabletops, silverware left on the kitchen counter. We found out later it was doing the equivalent of making itself comfortable, and moving things in some aggregate way, some extension of the sympathy one speck had for the others. I brought home a new Dyson, about five-hundred bucks worth retail. I fired it up and sucked and rolled the ball around chasing the dust. Though dust showed up in the whirlwind tunnels of the Dyson, the dust on the floor didn't decrease noticeably. Then we did all the other obvious things: called exterminators, enlisted the county extension agent, consulted with university professors (a mycologist and a DNA specialist). We took to the Internet to see if there were any references to it; there weren't. And the Internet searches came up crazy because there was no pattern to detect. We were experiencing the first one. So we knew it was new if the Internet didn't know about it yet. My son took on the job of telling the zeroes and ones.

Results: it was finer than talc; it could cause respiratory problems; its DNA was less interesting than its RNA; it wasn't a known fungus; the sympathetic movement between particles was clearly demonstrable but not explainable unless it was electromagnetic (but no charge could be detected). It didn't have a name (never mind order phylum, class, order, genus and species). It was alive only in the sense that the particles seemed to somehow know about each other, and the *knowing* part constituted for more than one scientist the designation of "alive." Another scientist quietly brought out two magnetic Scottie dogs, one black, the other white, put them together on the table and the one moved the other or joined with the other depending on the pole of its magnet. But the discussion didn't close there. The phenomena of moving objects—slowly, but nonetheless moving—was the final piece of evidence for sentience. It had mitochondria at the cell level, and it seemed very efficient at moving energy around in the cell walls.

Tendency to wander off here on the Christmas I actually received the magnetic Scottie dogs and what happened to them. So . . . irrelevant but, of course, in the big scheme of things an absolutely necessary part of the greater and ever-rolling story wherein all narrative possibilities are inseparable from each other. I always did have problems keeping them separate; it seemed so hemorrhaging clear that there was only one pool and we dipped all stories out of it.

My family and I moved out of the house by now. Each day the dust seemed to reproduce and, more exciting, apparently randomly move objects in the house. Eventually we found out what it was doing with the objects, moving them out of the way. But at the time one exterminator suggested burning down the house immediately before the dust got out. Get science people to save some in a jar, he suggested. Study it later in safe laboratory conditions. Fungicide fogs didn't work. What we also didn't know was that the white powder was waiting, getting things out of the way, setting up for the next stage.

The geneticists found that at one level, it had cells, but cells constructed differently from standard cells. The walls were very thin and seemingly much more fragile than normal cells, but they didn't depend on moisture to either maintain rigidity or pass genetic materials. So the RNA—the nuclear material, the instructions for the assembly of DNA (RNA is the is-ness, as one researcher said)—was fully running the cellular show, the ringmaster. And, as opposed to regular cells, these depended on dryness. If you wet them they didn't cease to exist exactly; they just turned to a kind of nucleic mud that waited to dry out to become active again.

My house has been sealed off as a biohazard until the state extension agents can get this under control. Under control seems to mean that they can name it. Name it and there will be a collective sigh of relief, apparently. They used gray tape around the windows and doors—a containment tape. The proposition of burning the whole thing to the ground is still valid. The pest control guy talked to the extension agent, and then they both talked to the police who called the university people. They called me in to check my insurance policy and that settled it. There was no pay off for purposely burning down the house even if the fate of the state, the earth, the universe was at stake. So unless the state went through the whole condemnation process, not to mention the compensation process, the house stayed. The dust stayed. Besides the containment tape, there was some kind of plastic goo they sprayed around all the openings to seal it further. They sent guys in biohazard suits to cut a viewing port in the living room wall. More sealing. That was followed by peering in, shining ultraviolet light in, and then low-grade radiation and some hush-hush strategies they wouldn't tell me about. I immediately realized I wouldn't be sitting in my living room chair any time soon—probably never. I waxed nostalgic. Why me? Alas. Alack. Like that. And more.

The dust—let's call it the new being—was reorganizing my living room by some kinetic agreement between its parts. The furniture was being arranged around the perimeter as if there was going to be a dance. Privately, because I didn't want my kids to hear this, I called it the "shit's happening" mode. The dust was getting ready for some serious hokey-pokey.

What did you think it would look like, an invasion from

space? Oh my God, we're not alone! Hell, we have never been alone, turns out. We've fallen in love with little green guys or the ones with the Spielberg finger pods phoning home. *Klaatu barada niktu*. But no, it came from Johnson Creek (try that out as a movie title) and I, well, my son and I, dumped bleach on it to bring it to life. For the historical record, it was my son's idea.

Personally, I was in favor of waiting for the dance to begin, so to speak. My furniture was all up against the walls and the dust growing deeper on the dance floor. Here's where the authorities say they're taking over. For the safety of the community. For the civilian population. For the love of God! I apparently was the only one for twenty miles around that was not assuming the dust had nefarious purposes. I suggested it just might want to say hello and then be on its way. That brought the suggestion that I seek some professional help at the counseling center. The words *contra naturum* came up. It would have to be destroyed because it was not natural and, I thought, but kept it to myself, that it was moving furniture around in a manner not sanctified by any local church or authority—not the sacred or the profane or the scientific community. Dust is one thing; moving furniture in an unnatural manner quite another. Augustine noted miracles were not so much against nature as against what was presently known about nature. Different thing altogether.

Authority, authorize, authentic, author: somewhere in the center of all these is the sense of power. Who gets to do what to whom? Who gets the last word? Who gets to peer through the viewing port at the new guy (Guys? Gals? I came quickly to favor *gals* and parthenogenesis, but maybe that's just because I'm a modern guy. Maybe because of the furniture moving). The government guy who took over had a tonsure of hair like a monk, wore a gray suit that exactly matched the containment tape (coincidence?) and a blue knit tie, a tie the likes of which I hadn't seen in twenty-five years. He had an assistant who carried a clipboard and smacked it on his thigh with gusto before raising it to write down what the authorized guy said he should write.

I know I can't keep this in but it was fun anyway—all the authority stuff. Dr. S is the author of Rex. Rex the author of . . . ? We'll find out, I'm pretty sure. And, right now, right here, I'm the author of all of them. I went farther into the country; there were sheep with letters stained on their sides—alphabet sheep. Is that a sign? A bunch of signs?

I began to see my house as a cosmic zoo. Maybe because I'd given up ever playing *Monopoly* again in my living room with the kids. Maybe because I was growing fond of the Holiday Inn the insurance company moved us in to: pool, spa, workout room, free continental breakfast. I thought it was time my people and I got together to name our houseguests, and maybe even welcome them. My eight-year-old thought this might make a fine class project at school, but we talked him out of it. Better keep it in the family.

Who knows, if we're friendly and the authorities piss it off, maybe we'll get to be the start of a new human race. So our gene pool has a little scum around the edges: some nut allergies, a little more than our share of insanity, that thing that grew on my grandma's chin, the great uncle who experienced what he called "angelism"—whatever that was—and the two-different-colored eyes syndrome that many people outside our family found charming. I, for one, would welcome some external vigor into our pasty gene pool. Some sentience that could move stuff around with dust and line up the furniture against the wall.

The jar my son took to school did the two things the visitor did to my house: the goo-to-dust transition, then the dust that could organize. Then, and I blame not poking holes in the jar (or whatever the equivalence of this act in the case of rapid mutation), the classroom jar went blank. I say blank because the elegant white of the dust in the house, that slightly violet cast that suggested vitality inside the dust, went out of the dust as if someone had flipped a switch. Some dust remained, but it was clearly dead and not organizing a damn thing.

In time the house observers noted that something happened in the cleared space in my living room. There were lines of peculiar arches like electromagnets make with iron filings. The lines were clearer in the dark and lit with black light they said. I kept my musings to myself, but I can report now that I immediately thought the dust might have set up some kind of discotheque—black light, cleared floor. That was a silly notion when I thought it. But now, I'm thinking maybe . . .

I used the term *visitor* a little earlier, but what I meant was visitor to my house, not visitor to the earth. I am more convinced each day that whoever they are, they are already here in constituent pieces. And we are the visitors, one in the possible arrangements of mad molecules flaunting our carbon.

You think?

Somebody at the university got an NSF grant to buy my house and land. They planned, I think, to seal up the whole thing and make it a study center with portals and safe rooms and protocols. A lot of protocols. I wasn't privileged to the whole proposal, just the big, fat check. I said, sure. Let me know how it works out.

I know now the real deal with the dust. I figured it out. And just after I cashed the government check, after the magnetic-looking lines occurred, the final stage happened. All the cell scientists noted the powerful exchange of energy within the cell. One told me that energy serviced by mitochondria schlepping back and forth for a piece of the food action, that energy was stronger than any he'd recorded. So here's what I think. It came together, it reorganized itself, and then decided, enough. Or maybe, enough already! Like when you play a video game for a while and you can kind of see where the whole thing's going and you quit. Like that.

My son thinks the lines were a landing field and whatever it was took off. Kids! He loved the dynamics of loading up and getting out of here. But I still think I'm right, and this whole business happens more than we care to admit: there's a new combo in town, it flourishes for a while, it goes extinct. I think rather than "goes" extinct, there are lots of them that just quit. Not all life forms have our yearning after reproductive success. I think the dust just smiled, said good enough, and waved goodbye.

Our new house is not on a creek. But the word is that there was a nineteenth century dump around here somewhere because the excavations unearthed some very small apothecary bottles and vials. It had the collectors out in droves. Some of the bottles had corks and bee's wax seals and liquid still inside. I like to think of these bottles as the next Johnson Creek floodwaters and my bottle of bleach. I'll keep an eye out and tell you how this works out.

Yeah, yeah, I know how much Dr. S business has crept in to this. It's the same goddamned story but let out on a different leash. The story is my voice that deals with what the world is telling me. How now brown Rex? I took me an extra hour to get home.

Chapter IV

The dust news item was a little sketchy but the final report had come in from the government and everything "had returned to normal," it seemed. Move along, apparently. Nothing to see here.

Marnie told me she had saved the piece because it seemed vaguely related to the stories I had told her about the good doctor. But what she really wanted to talk about was the new show she was installing—fractals made into art. I didn't see the connection at the time, but I do now—the fractals, that is, not the dust.

It seems—and I suspect that everyone has also suspected this at one time or another—that the natural world has a penchant for patterns. I found one guy, astronomer Arthur Stanley Eddington, who conversely said that these patterns were actually the manifestation of the human means of measuring. That is, there is no reality, just that what we find is a product of the means we have to search out and measure it—our own minds especially.

Here's the Wikipedia entry—a little more recondite, but to the point.

Sir Arthur Eddington wrote in his book *The Nature of the Physical World* that "The stuff of the world is mind-stuff."

The mind-stuff of the world is, of course, something more general than our individual conscious minds. . . . The mind-stuff is not spread in space and time; these are part of the cyclic scheme ultimately derived out of it. . . . It is necessary to keep reminding ourselves that all knowledge of our environment from which the world of physics is constructed, has entered in the form of messages transmitted along the nerves to the seat of consciousness. . . . Consciousness is not sharply defined, but fades into subconsciousness; and beyond that we must postulate something indefinite but yet continuous with our mental nature. . . . It is difficult for the matter-of-fact physicist to accept the view that the substratum of everything is of mental character. But no one can deny that mind is the first and most direct thing in our experience, and all else is remote inference."

—Eddington, *The Nature of the Physical World,* 276-81.

But most scientists and especially mathematicians, have found pattern after pattern. Fractals—especially Julia and Mandelbrot sets—are the designs made by a mathematical set of instructions (sort of like RNA). Color them any way you want, and you've got: art, algorithms made manifest in colors, the fingerprints of God, the face of God. More choices available. How about Dr. S's little set of instructions that come to lurk in an air-conditioned box in the Ag building? What little re-iterative algorithms are slouching toward Bethlehem to be born? Rex, as Dr. S described him to me, seemed to have a lot in common with the fractals—they were a set of repeating instructions.

So there's the tension—articles are always better with tensions: Eddington is on the money with his great extension of relativity—we see everything in the universe through the lens of human consciousness; the nature of neurons is the beginning of reality. Or . . . what I like to think of as the Robert Lewis Stevenson postulate: "The world is so full of a number of things, I'm sure that we'll all be as happy as kings." Said without irony, things are everywhere waiting for us to find or invent them.

These two camps have beautiful variations on the central themes. The bell curve is big and fat.

A second conversation with Dr. S, a number of weeks later when my article had grown way too long and lugubrious—the article that consumed itself and much of its surroundings. The article that was not to be, I came to think. The damn thing spread out and began to consume not only my every waking hour, but it sent tentacles in my wool gathering, my semiconscious day dreaming, my idle hours of writing up the article of the whole world.

I had found his office again, this time calling the animals by name, "Hi ya, Rosie. How's your udder?" And there sat Dr. S looking at graphs on his screen. In the corner was Rex, or so I thought.

I greeted the doctor and then greeted Rex with a wave and a hi.

"Correction," said my host. "That is not Rex. If you look closely, you'll see a kind of color variant on the original, Rex Prime. It's the same set of instructions but not the same critter. Very interesting. I kept thinking contamination of chemicals at first. CP, chemically pure, is only so pure, it seems. After the 99.99 percent is where the humor of the universe is located, apparently. Look at him."

We both went to Rex's lair and the doctor turned on a light. The blob was indeed both striated and speckled within the stripes like some rare African antelope only seen on Tuesdays under a full moon. So I asked what Rex II ate. And it seems the answer was also right out of Dr. Seuss: "Agar-agar."

"And some other stuff too," he said. "I see where you're going. He is what he eats. And eat he does. Did I mention that the remains, the feces so to speak, is just dust. He seems to metabolize very thoroughly. And look how slim he stays. I can put out food, really just dip him in it, and the food is gone and dust remains. I may have invented a perfect eating machine. I was going to give him a half slice of pepperoni pizza one day but thought better of it. I could make another one, of course, but it's a pain-in-the-ass long process. Rex Prime I think died for one of two reasons. He had either reached the end of his metabolic clock—got old and died per cellular instructions. Or—I somehow killed him with instructions or with food. Anyway, I keep Rex II on strict agar-agar to give him a fighting chance. What do you think? Should I start him on PB and J and then move up to pizza? Oh, and there's another possibility too. Rex Prime may just have left the premises, you know, like Elvis. I don't like to entertain what that one means, you know. He just got up and left? Got bored and is out there looking around for stuff to do? I hope not, but maybe . . . I am, after all, a scientist and must be open to all avenues that I haven't logically eliminated. Alas, there are all those NSF protocols about recombinant critters, protocols I didn't follow since Rex really wasn't a bacteria or virus. "

The doctor was in. And on. He had gotten into class-humor mode with me. And now there was no stopping him.

"So . . . What is it again, what you're interested in? You're doing an article on what?"

I wasn't sure. The whole business of Rex sulking in the corner, the Ag building alive with barn sounds, the goofy professor resigned to his hole-in-the-wall science, Marnie's fractal art somehow babbling up behind this stuff, my editor like some cigar-chomping Perry White fuming at Jimmy Olson, the entire R. L. Stevenson "happy as kings" line—ah, life at its best messiness, its beautiful messiness. I should have started with "left the premises."

I asked if I could photograph Rex, and Dr. S said yes, but no flash. I whipped out my phone and approached Rex still piled in the corner of his container like a stack of dirty laundry. "What's his good side?" I joked to the doctor. "Does he have a back side? Is it the same as his front? Could we un-pile him out of the corner?" I was used to the reporter's impertinence. It came easy to me now. The questions about how people feel in tragic situations, the question that goes over the line when people are fragile—all saleable, alas. The way of the biz, I figure. I couldn't have anticipated Dr. S's response.

"Okay, get the fuck out of here. I've had enough." It was the response many of my interviewees *should* have come up with but never did. The good doctor went right to the point. He figured I wanted to poke Rex with a stick—like enraging a circus lion to get a better picture. He didn't get my half-joke as I approached Rex with my invading lens. Or maybe, and here's the one I've come to think is the real reason I got told to fuck off: the parental instinct kicked in. Though the doctor had written the program and made a blob, it was *his* blob by God, his coded pile of genetic information. His child.

I left while trying to explain that I was only kidding, but the doctor wasn't buying it, or was sick of my intrusion or . . . yes, wanted to be alone with his creation, do whatever B horror-movie thing he did with Rex. Pygmalion, Eliza Doolittle. Slop some bleach on him and see what happens.

Driving home I thought of how I'd blown it. But blown what? Were there these guys all over the country making algorithms live? Was the whole basic-meat thing about to be solved, and Dr. S was only the recent snowfall on top of the tip of the iceberg? All kinds of speculative literature had been musing about this for the last fifty years. Then the scientific literature took over and began to show how some of the parts might be constructed. Mel Brooks made fun of it before it really happened—genius.

Maybe I should forget about Rex and go looking for the other ones that had to be out there. The scientific literature would have the keys to who was doing what experiments where. I felt the warmth of a trail—a journalist's wet dream just beginning. As I drove, I realized why no one was interested in Dr. S's paper at the conference—besides the sound system, that is—and the reason was that probably nobody there was doing this kind of thing. Make something sort of alive with lines of code to no particular end. And the corollary was that Dr. S had a room in the Ag building for exactly the same reason. No NSF or drug company money, no research assistant, no fancy apparatus. The doctor's equipment had looked exactly like the set of a very bad sci-fi movie: an oscilloscope, a centrifuge, a box or two with plenty of knobs, some kind of toaster oven to warm stuff, a refrigerator to cool stuff (and keep his lunch cold), some digital counters, books and detritus spread around so it looked like a mad-scientist's den. One chair. Maybe Igor was kept in cage back with the cows.

What I was pondering was the state of modern science whereby all experimentation of note was by definition very expensive and again, by definition, would be vetted by committees who doled out money, government or private, and defined what was worth doing, what was not—asking cowboys how sheep were to be shorn. The scientific paradigm was worth writing about. Dr. S was probably worth writing about but going to be difficult to recapture. The making of life was worth a shot but fraught with Frankenstein boilerplate. All these had different audiences, all had to be written in different styles. The question that has guided my career so far: Which direction should I take to get a paycheck and have some fun?

When I got home, Marnie made me shower and dress for the art opening. Once there I got my glass of cheap white wine and stood in my navy corduroy jacket with the elbow patches and was introduced to many clean faces. Everyone smelled nice.

But as I looked at the fractal art, I kept seeing versions of Rex. Rex at ease, Rex alert, Rex running through a graphics program like fairy in a field of daisies. I was reminded, standing there, that James Thurber's wife was reported (by him) to have jabbed him in the ribs as he stood at a party holding a glass of (cheap white?) wine looking out over the crowd, and after the jab she said, "Thurber, stop writing."

So I'm ruminating on reiterating polynomials, Julia and Mandelbrot sets, the stuff I picked up from the art opening—thinking about how time works in the generating of fractals, what the entry into the equation is for time (or distance? maybe). Early Mandelbrot sets were designed to approximate the coastline of England, and they looked just like the coastline of England. And I can't help thinking about Rex, his pouting in the corner and what this has to do with fractals, with anything. Somehow the two—fractals and Rex—have engaged me in that kind of "get shit done" mode I have as a writer of magazine articles. This thing over here talks to that thing over there. And if I listen in I get to hear what they say to each other, the connections, and report it. And while I'm again obsessing between these two poles, I remember another news item in the paper.

In Poland, in a factory settling-pond left over from the Soviet-era disregard for the environment, there appeared to several observers a sort of religious experience. While they sat and ate their lunches near the pond, the surface turned black, though the day was sunny and clear. Then after some minutes of perfect blackness, the surface of the pond turned gold, like gold foil used in the gilding process. And the gold stayed and stayed and stayed, until one worker stood up and heaved a rock into the gold. The splash erupted and gold flew up and gold rings pulsed out from the center. One worker later said the rock rose up suddenly and disappeared into the sky, but none of the others would bear him out on this account. The pulsing rings stopped then and the surface returned to gold for some minutes. Then suddenly it went back to the dun-colored waste pond they had known before. One of the workers, though it wasn't clear from the article if it was the same guy who saw the apotheosis of the rock, left immediately after announcing his life had been changed, and he was leaving to spread the word. He left so suddenly, the article went on, that his fellow workers didn't know exactly what word he was going to spread. There was discussion among the workers about what had just happened, what word there was to be spread. They agreed to a story that contained just the facts, the color changes, the rock, the leaving of their friend. Each one repeated it in nearly the same words as the others. Some outsiders came to set up a vigil near the pond, but the black to gold change didn't occur again. The end. XXX

Finally, while standing in front of an eight-foot by six-foot fractal colored by an artist (i.e. an artist *selected* the colors) but generated by a mathematician, I thought I heard the story of dust, the fractals and the story of black and gold all calling to me through my vision of Rex slumped in the corner of the cage. What is Rex doing? Rex I and Rex II, do you know the dust people? The surface of the pond and all its incumbent chemistry? Some fractals, it turns out, take the shape of dragons. Or shields, or coastlines. Or lumps of oatmeal whose surface is everywhere a reiteration of his shape at all levels of magnification. I'm going with "the fingerprints of God" for my behemoth article. It has that kick in the solar-plexus authority. Take that, Cosmic Mystery!

My voices: the last link that was also the first link. How's that tautology? As a kid, I had to sit in a room painted in desperate light green. It seemed hard to breathe, but I think that was just that I knew what was coming. The counselor ushered me into her office with all her patronizing concern torqued into her face. Eyes big in sympathy, brow furled in concern. Mouth held at neutral smile to make me feel . . . what? I remember feeling that I was about to be cheated out of something. Sold something I didn't want. I knew I had to stay with her and respond politely. But really I wanted to flee. Run and run and run until the drip of psych-babble peeled away from me in the wind. The counselor urged, and smarmed and solicited. "They went away," I finally blurted. "Maybe I was just . . . just hearing . . . somebody else talking to myself. I was talking to myself." When they finally let me be, I thought it was probably that moment, the talking-to-myself claim that set me loose. I stuck to it, and became a big fan of what I later called enabling fictions. The world is full of seams where we've stitched it together. Dr. S, the fractals, the fine dust. Rex was becoming a beautiful seam up the middle of my world.

Good boy, Rex.

I had run across the term "phenomenology" where it was defined as an ever larger umbrella so that when you thought you could see the edges of the umbrella, its gigantic spread and cover, well, then the umbrella got even larger. Suspend all judgment about whatever it is until all the information is in. It's never all in. Grow old and die. Then nothing will matter anyway. And that's where I found myself in the Rex-based conundrum: how is all this stuff part of the same thing?

Chapter V

Dr. S perched on the edge of his chair like an eagle overlooking his aerie. He saw me coming along the corridor but kept his perch until I rounded the corner into his office. "Rex has been asking for you," he announced. "He must have taken a liking to you somehow along the way. How's your article coming?" I waited for the repercussions of his last fuck-off, but they seemed forgotten. Or at least hidden. I wondered only briefly at the change of heart. I'd been doing this long enough to take what the interview would give me. Ask questions, be impertinent as needed, let them talk, and the article would write itself. I could assemble from any wreckage.

I was still parsing that Rex had asked for me, so I stumbled on the article question. "Fine. Yeah. No, not so good. What? Rex what?" I was going to try to avoid the sudden "fuck off" this time if I could. Once bitten. Behave myself, sort of.

"Well, I think he asked for you. You would be the 'question guy' he was referring to. He said, if I remember right, that we should let the question guy in on the talking. Something like that. You know how hard it is to understand goo." And then he cackled, a real cackle, and came out of the perch mode and sat in his chair. I wasn't sure what the hell or even what the fuck. I thought the doctor fully capable of jiving the shit out me at extended and profound depth, pulling my leg so long and hard that my arms would shorten.

Again I felt as if I had ended up in a Dr. Seuss story. *Speaking to goo, what would YOU do? Look! Look! You've got some goo on your shoe!* Cheese and rice, my old aunt used to say. Cheese and rice! But Dr. S seemed also sincere in his wish to introduce me to Rex. He took me by the hand and led me not to Rex himself but to a screen on a bench ten feet away from Rex. I glanced over at Rex heaped in the corner, stripes and all. I don't know why, but I waved. The doctor seemed animated by some internal fire, some compelling mania like a drunk hailing you too loud from across the room.

Dr. S started typing then stopped and ran a little program (as far as I could tell) and hit return. The wait was short. Dr. S turned to me and said, "Rex wants to tell you that though he's been out—whatever that means—he would like to come all the way out and meet more people. I think by being 'out' he means that some part of him—he used the word *spores* when we talked about this before—has already been out there. He said that actually it's been many, many times. Right since the beginning. First, by way of the animals here in the barn. Then later by me. Inadvertently, I assure you. And now he's proposing that you take him out there"—he waved toward the office door in general—"and, I don't know . . . meet people probably." Dr. S waved his hand expansively toward "out there somewhere" I guessed. But he also seemed perfunctory, distracted by something more important than introducing me to Rex again. If that was part of his put-on, he was a fine actor too.

I asked the doctor to explain what he had just input and what the program then did with it and what had come back and, of course, how it had come back. Right at this point I decided if I wasn't going to just slowly back out of here and run for it, then I was along for the ride whether the doctor was putting me on, was nuts or was getting signals from the other side or really speaking to the goo. I quickly decided that speaking-to-the-goo was the best story. The Ag barn today was also particularly full of voices: moo, bah, and in the distance, quack. My own personal barnyard lay silent, apparently waiting to see what would happen.

So here's what he told me: He writes the questions in a Word program (thanks, Bill Gates) and then he writes a little Python program to undo the words back into his own version of zeroes and ones—a version consistent with his original algorithm that is (was) Rex, the pile of goo that wants to go for a walk, apparently.

That's all. Nothing tricky except for the original formula (like KFC's secret herbs and spices, I figured). And he gets the answers back the same way, he said.

Now I am beginning to think I have at least two stories here. First there's Rex the . . . take your choice: talking dog, new life form, Pinocchio, alien who has abducted the poor old scientist. Second, there's the whack-job scientist who has now entered his own frustrated delusion so heartily that (Norman Bates rears his head here) his world is thoroughly infiltrated by his own madness and a new reality has taken over. All other versions, to this reporter, seem to be variations on these two themes. In any case, there's great stuff here and my job is to stay out of the way and let the story play out.

Rex apparently wants to talk to me more. The flying fingers of Dr. S are at first asking my questions to Rex and getting his answers. Then Rex starts to ask me questions. But he, like a ventriloquist through his dummy, asks them through Dr. S.

"Alfred," Dr. S reports. "Ask the young man what he thinks Rex is, what he thinks I am." And so Dr. S does. He asks.

I reply, "I was first thinking you might be sort of a talking granola bar warmed up and piped in through a computer screen." I had decided to go along with the Q&A format but keep a sort of snide skepticism to protect myself against the elaborate joke he might be playing. Fiction's layers.

"Then?"

I said, "Well, then . . . now, that is, I am pleased to report that I find you a highly intelligent and caring granola bar warmed up . . ."

"And piped through a computer screen?"

"Well, yes. That's how we're doing this, aren't we?"

"Would you be more comfortable if we did this more directly?"

"Would I have to eat something or hook up to something?" Let's recap so far: KFC, Norman Bates, and now Alice in

Wonderland.

"No, I'd do the hooking up," said Rex.

And then Dr. S stopped typing but I continued to hear the questions. "And now, is that more comfortable for you?" I was hearing Rex's tune directly on my nervous system.

Aye, there's the rub, Hamlet reported. Man who hears voices, again hears voices. I know. I know. But this had to happen. Which voices was I hearing? My own life-long companions—*my* team? Or just because the channels were nice and open in my particular case, was I susceptible to someone piping in outside voices? And finally, was this business, as Dr. S claimed, really Rex the oatmeal lump coming out to the world via a startled reporter? I refused to take my pick, opting instead for all-at-once no matter how conflicted the logic became. Not either/or, but both/and. In direct contact with Rex I am flooded with early voice strategies. Having escaped the counselor's suffocating empathy in my youth, I concocted ways to not respond to the voices, even the startling one that just called my name. I wanted to scream: "Does everything have to mean something? No no no no," etc.

"So. What would you like to see invented?" Rex said in my head.

I did a kind of mental double take to get into the mental-only mode. "Say what?" I said out loud. Dr. S laughed and said (out loud), "You don't have to say it you know."

So I tried just thinking it, and Rex apparently got everything. He said, "Just what I asked. What would you like to see in the coming years? Let's just jump over world peace and harmony—not that it's off the table, but everything in its good time; there would have to be some MAJOR adjustments for that to happen and there'd be resistance like you wouldn't believe to the preconditions to world peace. So let's just get on with it."

Rex's voice was very like my other voices, I'll admit, but had more continuity, more gravitas. I was reaching. More sincerity, maybe. Harder to ignore with my blah-blah-blah rejection. It was something like when you put one earbud in and then add the other and the stereo kicks in and the voice happens right in your old medulla oblongata and surfing upward.

"Flying cars?" I proffered to give myself more time. And right away the Jetsons flew through my mind—all of them in their flying car with their dog, Astro. I felt trapped in a moment of Dr. S's making. What was he doing to manipulate me? How was he pulling this off? Where oh where was the center of this experience: in my head, in the computer, in the bowl of goo? "Nice one. Yeah. That's going on the list." Rex somehow managed to have me understand that he was rolling his eyes. "And . . . ?"

This was kind of fun, though. I had been preparing for this my whole life. No freaking out, just listen to the voices. The voice. But the odd part was having an observer, Dr. S. It was like having someone watch you have sex. There he sat smirking while I talked with Rex. Clearly, Dr. S was not hearing either side of the conversation.

I went on. "Okay, so I'd like to charge my phone and iPad without hooking up to wires. Maybe just lay them on a device and they'd be charging. Oh, and then, maybe getting rid of all electric wires for transmission of power. That would be done with the new device that would send the power in packages, maybe radio waves, to be stored in—while you're at it—some new kind of batteries that would not discharge by themselves, would last forever if they're not being used. Got that?"

"Okay. That's better."

Dr. S was slouching in his chair with his legs swinging back and forth, and he was grinning like the Cheshire cat. That cat was an apropos image, given that I was talking to a bowl of striped, sassy oatmeal. Funny I don't remember smoking anything, unlike Alice. Jefferson Airplane joined the cacophony in my frontal lobes, and then some other lobes too. "One pill makes you bigger, one pill makes you small. And the pills your mother gives you don't do anything at all. Go ask Alice . . . when you're ten feet tall." The whole business was seamless in my head—music, questions and answers. It felt as if my head were filling like a glass of water where the noise rises in pitch as the glass fills. The whole shebang was simultaneous, one thing on top of the other but distinguishable multitasking. Good boy, Rex.

Rex went on. "And what else? Maybe something in the health-care line?"

"Sure. How about viruses that could be trained to attack cancer growths, and *just* cancer growths, and then after they took out the cancer they'd fly up their own assholes and disappear from the bloodstream. Like Doberman Pinschers. But with the asshole-flying-up part added. Or . . . or the viruses just unmask the cancer and your own immune system takes over."

It wasn't exactly a laugh. But then I didn't really hear it either. But the laugh idea was there in the layers going on in my head. I had made Rex laugh. Dr. S asked me if Rex laughed. I should tell him if I made Rex laugh. I held up one finger and said I just had done exactly that.

"He must like you," said the doctor, "although I'm not sure what there is to like in such a one as you." I allowed as how I found that true myself once in a while. Rex was undeterred.

"That's not bad, and not that hard to do, either. There are people already messing around with this. What they don't have is the knack to address the virus critters. They're just a couple steps away. I should probably shoot one of them the way to do that—maybe a dream like Kekule's snake with its tail in its mouth—the benzene ring."

"So, wait. You've been around for a hundred years?"

"No, I was just cooked up by my associate here. Oh, the time thing. All I'll tell you now is: Negotiable! The whole time thing's negotiable. Was, is. Go went gone. Now the subjunctive—that's much closer. Contrary to fact, wished for, yearned after but written with a tweak to the grammar as if it is—was, were. But that's a whole 'nother kettle of fish,' as my doctor friend here says."

Dr. S nods vigorously, and I wonder if he actually is in on the conversation. But then I think he's just cheering me on somehow.

"Let's see," I say, just to get on with it. "Let's talk about feet. Ankles too. I see so many old folks hobbling around and sometimes they'll say 'knees' if I ask. But mostly they say feet, and ankles. Could we do something about the feet in pain?"

Rex, I think, pauses. "You see, there you've got another one of those deals where we'd have to change so many other things that there'd be an uproar, a revolt, even though the pain in the feet would be gone. Here's the rub: the original design—Darwin notwithstanding—is still the standard for humans. Bone density, soft tissue, damnable ACLs and all that, those were meant to last about thirty-five years, long enough to breed and then die and get out of the way. So you take this basic model and you stretch it to eighty years . . . what the hell do you expect? Even the best ones are worn out at double the original thirty. So we can go back to the beginning . . . ah, see, this is where you get the resistance, of course. But what you really want is *the dip*. I've been thinking, the feet, cancer stuff, and all the rest of the mistakes bodies start to make after a while, all this could be fixed with a regularly scheduled dip. You'd go in to the shop every six weeks or so—I've got a longer version too, but I think the six-week interval is good. Keeps people aware of the repairs and doesn't let any of the mistakes get much of a start on the body. So, you'd go in and for a fee—tied to the price of basic cable so that anyone could afford the dip by canceling cable for a month—you'd take off your clothes and get dipped in the fixer. I know there's a better name out there but it hasn't come to me yet. The fixer goo—get that heel too, Achilles!—would reset all the little biological errors and you'd be good to go. How's that sound?" The "mistakes" business, the cell failure, the built in obsolescence—all had a familiar ring from his class lecture. Dr. S, are you there? Am I talking to a puppet?

I say, "Goo? Does it have to be goo? Couldn't it be like an aromatic spray, maybe with a little rosemary oil or . . . I've got it, the smell of a baby's head. Sure, and there'd be a mist in a shower stall, then you'd walk out. Is goo really necessary?" I found myself shifting in my seat, tugging at an earlobe, scratching my nose. Outside the wind was blowing and the barn smells shifted and seemed all flowing through the doctor's office—cow, sheep, chicken, horse, cow again. Rex is breathing.

"Here's the reasoning behind the goo. Every six weeks you'd have to make a decision to get the goo all over you, a kind of commitment, that would, well . . . commit you, see what I mean? It couldn't be too easy or pleasant or people would be in there lining up for a naked dip every week or ten days. Nope, it's got to be an event. The goo makes it an event."

"So, is this negotiable too? Like time?"

"Actually, everything's negotiable—like time. Taxes, death, war, tides, gender, glaciers—all negotiable too. You people are pretty slow about this. Pretty slow about way too many things, actually. But, as I said, we'd have to change some basic structures to change these. And nothing pisses off humans more than changing the basic structures. Alien invasion! they yell. Zombies! Jesus, Mary and Joseph, you people can't grasp the basic principle that's in front of your noses every day—when you change one thing, *everything changes*. It's a *fucking* spreadsheet, man! Darwin already told you."

I could see Rex was getting pretty worked up all of a sudden. I'm still not sure what set him off, but I thought the interview was probably getting to the end for today. My head was filled and overflowing out my ears. He had tagged up in all of my lobes by now. Did he just call life a fucking spreadsheet? Was he heading toward giving me the brush off the same way Dr. S did? The sudden get-the-fuck out of here? I have to admit to no fear, no substantial weirding out, no discomfort or malaise of any sort. I could keep this up. Bring on more voices, bring in a Souza band, bring in NASCAR in the background. I'd been training for this all my life. Bring in the *King Lear* storm and the battle of the Maginot line and the kettle calling the pot . . .

But I say, "Okay. Okay. Just one more thing then. If I make up a full list of things to change—feet, cancer, viruses, electrical storage, all that stuff, will you give me some kind of plan we could maybe work on, a little at a time?"

"You're not listening to me. You're not listening to me. Are you? Why aren't you listening to me? What part of this whole 'fix it' business don't you understand? That one thing changes everything? Or that no one wants everything changed? *Anything*, really."

Agitated, I'd call it. He was agitating the inside of my head until I felt his agitation and the cosmos knocking on my brain door. Here was salvation for all humankind, but he was agitated, pre-pissed off at us all. Take that Jesus. Salvation and surcease from pain all at his sticky, gooey fingertips, and Rex can't keep his oatmeal-shit together. The barn now in sympathy sounds like some crescendo of the "Halleluiah Chorus." Rex, quack, moo, grunt, Rex, cluck, and the waves of sound inside and outside my head seem to weave themselves together. And the barn smells, the swinging legs of Dr. S. like a large child, the orange glow of Rex's Lucite box, the hum of the computer hard drive that's now louder and louder—I am filled up, thorough. Completed.

* * *

Doctor S said quietly that we should turn down his light now, set his heat a little lower and give him a rest. He had a tendency to "heat up" and also grow himself out of his food supply. Dr. S claimed that the food supply was the only real control in this experiment. And if Rex somehow became able to get his own food, well, the experiment part would be over and the next stage would be delivering ourselves from an angry god—old story.

Every culture had some version. Not good times, those angry-god stories.

I sat in the car afterward wondering what the hell I had just been though. The fact that I had been doing voices in my head for as long as I could remember couldn't quite contain what I'd been through. When I asked Dr. S if he had conversations with Rex he said that he did, "sort of," and that he wouldn't really call them conversations. Maybe more like mind nuzzles. He used the word "nuzzle." Dr. S asked me what kind of nuzzle I had got from Rex, and I, of course, wasn't going to tell him a damn thing, same as I had always told people in white coats. I told him it was sort of a foggy connection. Dr. S gave me *nuzzle*; I gave him back *foggy*.

Rex, at this point, seemed to me an amalgamation of leftovers from all my life, some kind of psychic breaking of great wind. Was all that futuristic stuff just the sloppy leavings of my own concerns? I have always thought there's a kind of mind-sump that Freud never really got to, the dregs down there you really didn't want to stir up very much. The stuff that should just be left alone. Bird calls from the thicket, you know. Just leave them. My metaphors chased each other round and round until they tired, and I drove babbling home.

* * *

The fractal art was still up at Marnie's gallery. There would be several "openings" for the show—Thursday, Friday and Saturday nights—to sell the art. Red dots on the description of each piece indicated "sold." I learned from Marnie that sometimes galleries would put on the dots even if a piece wasn't sold—usually on the least likely to sell—just to make the others seem more desirable. Apparently, the shill worked. Red dots everywhere. Marnie schmoozed. I stood in the middle again with the cheap, white wine lubricant. Rex wouldn't leave me alone.

After I left Rex and Dr. S in the barn, I wondered how duped

I was. Did the mad doctor fiddle the whole adventure on his computer? I had to admit that I preferred my own adventure to having a psychokinetic blob that could pre- and post-cognate with me on my own nervous system—marvelous bullshit that sounds like. But I had to admit also that I was fully aware that the doctor knew that I was writing an article bound to be read by the same community he felt might shunt grant money his way, and he was perfectly capable mentally of outthinking us all for any given period of time. He could well be at the end of his intellectual rope: first he thought his work itself would get him the money to continue, then he found out nobody gave a shit unless there was a "wow factor." Enter Rex, vocal and magnificent.

I turned from one fractal and noticed there were the symmetric ones and the asymmetric ones. I read the labels and they were respectively based on Mandelbrot and Julia sets. These mathematicians made what might be thought of as the RNA of the art, the set of instructions for the raw materials—the DNA of color. The fractals were consistent—the same—on all scales so that if you zoomed in, or even looked very closely, you could see the repetition. The label used the word "iteration." To me they looked like garishly colored islands seething with color and then kaleidoscopic. Fractals were designs that the art world had snatched from the mathematicians and then tarted up. Math equations going to the prom. High drag for maps (I was searching), stony 70s movies in stop frame. Psychedelic algebra. Yikes!

And that set me off back to Rex. Was Rex an iteration? Dr. S set him off with the original algorithm and that set of instructions got parlayed through some polynomial equation of the doctor's into loquacious but unstable Rex. And what did Rex mean by using me to get around and see the world? I could feel myself over wrought and overwriting as if Rex had left skid marks on the underwear of my brain. Rex the infinite iteration of a simple gob of algebra. What would a Rex fractal look like? Would he choose his own colors? These math sets that hung on the gallery wall were really just concoctions, group efforts as slick as five-color printing could negotiate. Rex the same?

Marnie was at my side watching me watch.

"Which one do you like best?" she hummed.

"Trick question? You know I like you the best." Small points scored but that's how to build up the big score. I got a breast squeezed into my arm for my effort.

"No, you know, the art?"

I pondered, as if I hadn't already made up my mind and assigned Rex's name to one of the art pieces. "The blue one," I answered, though there were a couple of different blue ones. But one was BLUE, an unnatural blue that faded in and out across the shape that contained it. It exploded on the canvas, like LED lights in a Christmas string, like God's eyes out of which blasted seraphim in gales of pure love. Like . . . She knew immediately which blue one I was talking about. I asked, "How does the artist get that blue?"

She laughed. "Remember when you had 256 colors on computers? Then more and more and now a computer can do infinite variations on colors, some variations so small you can't tell the difference unless you look at the designation, the formula. This artist is very good at playing the computer."

"Like God on the very first day? Pretty much fun."

"More like an artist in an electronic studio fiddling the dials."

I loved the way she said "fiddling" and told her so. She used to think I was not taking her seriously when I said things like that. But now she knows I take her more seriously than I take anything in the world. That's love, I guess. "When you say 'fiddling' my whole spine goes soft. You know that, don't you?"

"No more wine for you. I'm cutting you off." She pushed me away and made her way off toward a potential customer who came for the art and wasn't always thinking of new ways to get in her pants.

I pondered the blue. The BLUE. The blue that was everywhere in the piece of art but nowhere in the world. And there was Rex again.

It wasn't the wine, either. Rex was recursive, reiterative, infinitely regressing—everywhere the same. He had to be. Dr. S had said about the instructions that made Rex, "I just wrote the basic string, and then Rex repeated it until it was enough." Enough what? I had asked. "Enough information, I think," the good doctor said.

And it was the "I think" part that had bothered me at the time, the lack of a scientist's control. The guessing part in the face of not enough information to understand what exactly he'd done by creating Rex. On the other hand, there was a distinct possibility that Dr. S knew *exactly* what he was doing right from the get-go. That was scarier, maybe, but not as interesting a narrative line (really just the old mad scientist story). The other story, that Rex had taken over once he had "enough information," that was money. The newspaper the next day gave me the idea it had turned out to be the later.

Maybe Rex was just fooling around—playing. The newspaper article noted that an industrial painting company reported that it had finished painting an entire trucking company with a combination of colors, reflective silver for the rooftops and an easy-to-clean bluish gray for the walls with a slightly darker blue trim. The color scheme was worked out ahead of time with the help of a computer simulation and the approval of the company's board of directors. When the painters finished, overnight the colors had changed. At first they suspected some kind of sabotage, some tricky paint mixing by a disgruntled employee. But they inspected the empty cans, the sprayers, interviewed workmen, ran tests, prodded and poked, and still there was no explanation as to why: the roof turned beet red, the walls a deep Mediterranean blue, and trim bright yellow—a gigantic Mexican restaurant. It looked altogether like an enormous and expensive prank by a Cristo-like artist who was trying to comment on the military industrial complex. Maybe assault by pigment. I don't know why—probably the art show the night before—but immediately I thought of Rex saying he wanted to get out more.

I imagined how the second Rex interview would go. This was a longstanding practice of mine, an interview technique really. I thoroughly imagined not only my own questions for an interview but the answers too. Then, listening carefully during the interview, I would redirect the parts that didn't fit my imagined answers, and that often led me to what I called "the good stuff."

"So . . . Rex, how you been?"

"Not so bad, yourself?"

"Been out and about, have you?"

"Some. Why do you ask?"

"Thought maybe you wanted to try a little *en plein air* painting."

And here I imagine he goes into a recitation of how colors are actually not what we see with our human eyes. For example, trees are actually blue and humans are seeing the reflected light or what the tree leaf is *not* when we say the leaf is green. It's blue. It's blue and that's what you mean to say when you say it's green. The leaf knows. Computers know. Scientists actually know this. But you persist in saying it's green."

"It's the yellow trim on the trucking company that I'd like to discuss."

"Yellow to you, anyway."

And this conversation goes on like this, I imagine, until Rex overheats again and Dr. S has to lower his light, lower his temperature. Of course the real burning issue here is, how. How did Rex get out (A) and (B) how did Rex change the colors?

I thought the best strategy would be to look around the paper for more signs that Rex had been out playing. Immediately I found in the newspaper another, then another, then another. I realized that the following all qualify: lady finds all her garden gnomes are missing and they turn up on a monastery lawn fifty miles away; eight-year-old drives his parents' car to visit a cousin in a town twenty miles away; cheese maker finds in his aging cave that one of the bigger cheeses has "eaten" all his smaller cheeses; and, well . . . insert assorted world-weirdnesses here.

Postulate: Rex out playing actually made more sense of the world than just considering the world without Rex.

Now that was a service to mankind: angels, ghosts, transubstantiation, starfish plagues where they all turn to mush, Ouija boards, Madame Blavatsky, phantom rickshaws, the monkey's paw . . . okay, I digress. But there it is—an oubliette down which we can chuck all the unexplained.

I had written myself completely out of an article. Too big a rubber bag. But Rex remained, and certainly another interview was in order. I was pretty sure I didn't now have any idea what the actual story would be. Maybe I should have told more people about the voices.

I promised Marnie that I'd just be obsessed with this for a couple days. A kiss for luck. Then another. It was nice that neither of us worked regular hours. Then another.

I wrote in my head the preliminary interview the way I always did. In the Ag building past the now familiar cows and sheep—hi there, guys and gals—I went straight to Dr. S's cave. It wasn't there. He wasn't there. His office and lab had been repurposed as a storage facility piled with sacks of grain, shelves of chemicals, a tack room. I double checked to make sure where I was. And wither goeth Dr. S, there goeth Rex. Ruth in the alien corn.

I pursued my new tangent by seeking out the power position of the secretary who seemed to know everything. The high priestess, I thought of her. She told me that the doctor and his lab had new digs now actually in the biology building. So down the halls past chemistry emergency washing stations, around the corner where ranks and file of offices were beset by slouched students impaled on their earbuds, then across a sky bridge and the errant molecules of formaldehyde announcing bio and biochem and micro-bio and the thrumming home of an electron microscope. All these replaced the chickens, cows and sheep. I wandered in the new maze listening for Rex on my nervous system, hoping I might tune in on him unaware, sneak up on his algorithm so to speak. No such luck. I rambled down the assigned labs the secretary had told me about. I looked for the "big one" she said Dr. S had been assigned, but they were all small. And then, there . . . there it was, the reward for his having made great scientific strides, I guessed. A palace of a lab. A Xanadu of a lab.

Fit for a Rex, I thought. But I kept hearing the word, "perturbation," while standing outside, waiting for an audience with them both. Maybe I was hearing it through the glass. I knocked. It should, by rights, have been a dark and stormy night. But the office was well lit, well ventilated, well appointed. I knocked again. The doctor had a graduate assistant who came to the door to ask my business: a clean, nice-smelling, bright-eyed female in a lab coat with "Joan" blue-stitched on, the university's name beneath. It all smacked of NSF money and proper sufficiency of garb, of equipment, of etiquette.

"I'm interviewing Dr. Sewall," I said, as importantly as I could.

"I'll see if he has time to talk to you. Do you have an appointment?"

Appointment? I thought I might stop and scratch a Holstein's ear before I talked to him, ask a sheep how it is to be shorn. "No," I said. And she just-a-minuted me.

I was left in the anteroom listening for Rex piping his song. Are you there, Rex? I asked. "Perturbations," came back again.

When Dr. S came out to give me an audience, he was remade: haircut, Ralph Lauren tie with little sailboats on it, better lab coat than Joan's with more writing on it, and the shoes: slick brown Italian jobs that purred. All accomplished in just a few days.

Wow.

"Doctor Sewall, I presume," I opened with. Nice shoes would have been my second choice.

"Ah, the young man with the inquisitive habits," said the doctor. I thought there was also some hint of a British accent, some kind of John Cleese put-on. "What can I do for you today?"

Where to start? He sat down in a chair like any old human being. Then he offered to have his assistant get me tea or coffee. He dangled one brown Italian over a knee. He might have had a peel and scrub. He glowed. "Could I continue my interview with Rex?"

Dr. Sewall laughed. "Rex has been in a kind of secretive mode recently. He reports that he's spending a lot of energy on outside projects, and he, well . . . *demands* more and better food."

"Sounds like an unhappy prisoner."

"Young man, Rex is no prisoner. If anything, *we* are the prisoners. All this is his world." The doctor waved expansively around the room, but I suspect he meant something larger than just these digs. Rex, by the way, was nowhere in sight, and I kept sneaking peeks around to see if there was a box of goo in some corner or other. Far away a siren, just audible, wailed and wailed. I should have seen it as a sign. It seemed to me that Dr. S was speaking through layers of gauze to me, through some kind of chicane maybe in which mirrors delivered his speech from some far away fortress. He continued, "I ought to mention that I'm not sure exactly what number Rex we have by now. Remember the addition of stripes. It seems that stripes was some kind of 'choice' Rex made, sort of sartorial, like wearing an ascot. I use the term 'choice' advisedly, though. Same caveats apply as in our original interview. On the other hand, you see the changes around you, I assume." He swept to the office with his hand. "Somebody up there likes Rex now. And the manna comes raining down." He rained manna high to low with waving hands.

I was watching him talk, like someone had taken the old Dr. S out of the Seuss book and put him in a Tolstoy novel, the world-weary Anna Karenina just before she jumps in front of the train. And it occurred to me, siren fading now, that Rex had somehow melded with the doctor in order to get his "better food." At least that was what I hoped. What a hell of a story that would be. *The talking oatmeal leaps the bonds of goo-hood and occupies the body of a scientist—his own father.* The Invasion of the Body Snatchers meets Frankenstein, meets The Blob, meets the Borg meets Keanu Reeves just back from the Matrix. Jeez, this is good stuff.

"Well, is there any way I can still talk to Rex?"

"I think you can, but the question is will *he*? He seems to think, and again 'think' is used with a looseness I can only begin to hint at, he seems to think he's said what there is to say. And then there's that other set of conditions you were witness to—the anger, the overheating, the outstripping his food supply. He may have solved that problem without commenting on the fact." The doctor sighed and looked at his significant watch, some kind of ten-grand Piaget. I was getting the feeling of approaching a carousel on which the horses and other animals had begun to squirm off their poles and eye me. Ride anyone?

"I'd like to try, though, just for old time's sake."

"Go ahead." And the doctor got up and opened a door to a dimly lit room. In a corner similar to his original corner in the Ag building, was Rex in his Lucite box with holes poked in it like a bug jar in some kid's bedroom.

I gave it a shot: leading questions (both thought and aloud), accusations about his messing with life forms many hundreds of miles away, then the pastiche of movie clichés, how he'd come to occupy the doctor's body, re-coloring the trucking company, and finally insults about his coloration and loss of stripes and dull brown coat. Nothing. I had persisted long enough to begin to feel more than a little foolish talking to a brown lump in a plastic box. Someone *has* to be filming this for a PBS special. I whipped out my cell and filmed the blob. I pretended to upload everywhere, ticking them off—Instagram, Facebook, Pinterest, Twitter, etc.—to see if I could get a rise out of Rex. Silence. Then silence broken by the doctor laughing behind me.

"See? Rex has gone to the proverbial cave at the top of the mountain that we see in so many *New Yorker* cartoons. We must make a pilgrimage to him. Sacrifice, trial, travail, hardship—we must pay a price for audience. Especially sacrifice, I think. And then, maybe, enlightenment."

Was that the doctor talking, or Rex? The blob wasn't talking. It sulked, I think. Like a grouchy teen. He looked no bigger, no better than the last time. The doctor laughed again. I offered: "Maybe you should stop feeding him and see if that gets him to break his silence. He'll blab like crazy if he's hungry enough."

The doctor smiled and led the way back into the lighted rooms. His watch gleamed again. "Now why would I endanger my own project? Stop feeding him. Good one. I haven't fed him in six weeks. I put the food out, but I think he's gone beyond food. Or he's taking miniscule amounts and metabolizing it fantastically, getting energy from next to nothing. Maybe like an air plant, some kind of orchid. I weigh the food carefully and it seems to remain all there. But he could be taking such small amounts that..."

Doctor Sewall was leading me toward the door to the anteroom where he'd hand me to Joan who'd show me out. But I wasn't done yet. I had feeling that I was being bum-rushed away from the best and weirdest story and/or hoax that I would ever encounter as a journalist. Pulitzer. Is there a Nobel for journalism?

And I was out the door with the lovely Joan schlepping me toward my reward—a cup of espresso freshly brewed and my choice of flavor syrups.

"Joan," I asked. "Does Doctor Sewall have any other journalists visiting him? Other colleagues working on his experiments with him? Co-authors on his papers?"

Joan smiled and tugged her new lab coat straight. "I don't know," she said, as if pondering that particular string of language for the first time.

While Joan concocted coffee, I sat in the waiting room and picked up a newspaper. I was attracted by a brief "bus plunge" article, you know, the kind that in one line declares that a "bus plunged" off a cliff in India, Mexico, Indonesia, etc., and everyone in the wedding party, school outing, family picnic was killed. I had a friend who collected these in a scrapbook. But below this brief article was an expose of the local meatpacking industry featuring a sausage maker not indicted by a grand jury but cited for careless and unsanitary practices in his company.

I took the coffee with me. Joan smelled nice and bid me out the door. On the way to my car, I first calculated my next move with Dr. S. How did I get into the *sanctum sanctorum* where he pulled strings and arranged the mirrors and stoked the smoke machine? "What dreams may come when we have shuffled off this mortal coil . . ." occurred to me first; bless you Hamlet. Then I began to process the sausage company and Rex with my populated writing world. In the car, stuck in traffic, the resolution came.

I moved Dr. S over one notch on the belt of weirdness. What would that be? A hit man. I wrote in the car again, this time in traffic. The Hit Man:

He had been trying to get to sleep for over an hour. He used his old tricks: thinking of childhood times and places, thinking of stationary objects like bridges he had known, thinking of flowers—fields of flowers, no wind. How could anyone get to sleep counting moving sheep? But the old tricks didn't work. And so he embraced the awakeness like a stranger in the room he was somehow forced to talk to.

There was no reason to stay awake. He had killed a person before and slept beautifully. And the other nights. Every time. It couldn't be that business—that's what it was, business—since he rarely even thought about any victims again once he was sure all his traces were obliterated. He admitted to himself that other people seemed to have a circuit he didn't. He saw the premise in movies and TV shows that the killer was tortured by his conscience (or something) and driven to foolish acts by remorse (or something) and often caught by his own inability (or something) to hide his deed. The entire logic of so many movies depended on it: war movies, accidental deaths, greed and revenge killings—so many kinds of killings. He thought: there is only the one kind. The making-someone-dead kind.

Once the initial twist had been made and the doctor properly mutated into fiction, the thing took off. The traffic slowed into stop and go. Like a sentence.

The world was infested by human beings carving out every day more and more miserable existences in caves, under the roots of trees, in sewers—even if all these places were called by the names of the great cities of the world. To him it really didn't matter at all one more or less. They were alive then they were dead. The formula was simple. He would also be alive, then dead.

That's how I'd begin it. Listen to ***that*** *voice for a while. The traffic had me unstuck in a temporal line—going nowhere, needing nothing, helpless. I played on . . .*

Robert was tall and thin and an unlikely looking killer. It was, he felt, a convenience that he looked like a vacuum cleaner salesman, a middle school principle, an accountant. Those movie killers were somebody's idea of what a "professional killer" looked like. Killing was really just a series of inventions and then the final act. The real difficulties always lay in dealing with whoever purchased the death, making a clean break with the client well before carrying out the deal. He had once waited six months for the proper window and conditions before delivering the promised death. Everybody wanted something right now. That was first in negotiations: Robert must own the time schedule or there was no deal. There would be no timely political assassinations (still the same kind as all the others) in which everything was on a clock. Find someone else for *that* business. In one case, the customer had insisted that a certain day would be the day, some kind of anniversary, and Robert had refused the commission right from the initial negotiations. The time must be flexible: plans could change like weather, conditions could alter by a flat tire, a stalled bus, a local fire, a case of diarrhea.

The police would admit to a large number of unsolved murders, and lurking behind those numbers an even larger number concealed from the public in the name of civic confidence in the police force. Robert's favorite made-up plots were two: (1) beaten to death with a frozen leg of lamb and then the murder weapon cooked and eaten (and served to the family in the spirit of the house of Atreus)—a Rod Serling plot, and (2) spears of water frozen and then fired into the victim with compressed air. He thought about all the ways people could die, and still he couldn't sleep. All those pedestrian accidents that weren't accidents. The heart attacks, strokes—all chemically undetectable, all acts of God. So God could murder but people couldn't? Really? Oh, yeah, well there was war, of course. Anyone could murder then in the name of oil, land, revenge for historically located acts, for relieving long pent-up hatred that no one could remember the reasons for. So why couldn't he sleep? It had been six hours since his last cup of coffee. Could the caffeine stay in his system that long? Hemingway called hunting the "gift of death" for the birds. The gift. The gift. The gift. The gift. And Robert was asleep.

Some of that wandered but was still within range of keeping. And anyway, it was all for a good cause—keeping focus on Dr. S and his now-elusive Rex. I thought of elusive kings in history and went back to the story as the asshole in front of me decided to change lanes though that one wasn't moving any faster than my lane. My theory is that lane-changers just get bored and do the whole crunch-over thing just to be doing something in the soul-cleaving experience of traffic jams. A siren in the distance again.

The glass and steel of the buildings seemed to amplify the rain, repeating each drop and catching the blow and simmer of the storm. On the street, there were blank pockets of dry caused as the conformation of a building where it broke up the swirling wind and made islands in the flow. Robert stopped in one such dry spot just behind a courtyard piece of statuary almost two stories high that created its own umbrella. The rain fell around him as if he had a charm protecting him, a spell, the finger of God.

All these people walking around. Live people but each one with: (1) a price tag—what are their lives worth? Their deaths? And (2) an expiration date when the live/dead business took care of itself. Shelf life. Sooner or later. The one or the other. There used to be a mac-and-cheese place around here somewhere, he thought. And he walked slowly out of the rain shadow toward a diner across the street that might have been that very same mac-and-cheese place. Never work hungry.

Background. This was the interesting part—invention out of thin air but with a fine, invisible thread that dragged one piece of the story after another through the treacherous scree scattered across the slope of story.

Robert Neff, he had researched the name and it had been *pont neuf,* and then Ellis Islanded into Neff. He smiled to think his relatives had been disease-free, able to work and of upright character as they lined up to be de-loused as a symbolic gesture: Europeans required de-lousing to become Americans. Let the louse stand for all else that must be killed off, pared away. His father sang to him the last vestige of the family Frenchness: *Sur le pont, d'Avignon, on ni danse, on ni danse . . .* and then had shown him the picture of the bridge at Avignon that ended halfway over the river, a bridge good only for dancing, not getting anywhere. Robert loved that his people had written a song about the bridge, but never fixed it.

There were a number of difficulties keeping a female friend. At first he could remain mysterious, what he did exotically distant, and it actually helped with attraction. But very quickly he found himself defending himself against female curiosity about how he made his living. Was he in some secret part of the CIA that wouldn't allow him to talk about work? Just in general, what kinds of things did he have to do in order to get a paycheck? And then the evasiveness itself became divisive. Don't you trust me? Love is trust. I would never tell anyone anything. And so he tried paying for female company, very expensive female company: discrete, compliant, prompt to come and go (so to speak). And that seemed to work as far as the body was concerned. He had found one girl—whom he tipped very well—who was almost like a girlfriend on retainer, a convenience of some significance in his life. He liked her out to the powerful edge of what the word meant. He thought about her when she was absent, he was always glad to see her, he found himself trying to make her laugh because when she laughed, he felt good. She canceled with other clients when he called. She filled in his life right up to major holidays and then again after.

This arrangement worked well until the time she canceled on him. And he quickly figured out she had found a better deal, and he had been relegated to second-class citizenship in her world. Idly, he thought of killing his competition but not out of jealously; after researching the concept he didn't think he felt anything remotely like jealously. But quickly he realized he could just find another girl and that the real proposition had been an economic one—the new guy tipped better than Robert, he made her laugh more, he made more appointments. It was business and if Robert wanted her services he would have to compete at the dollar level. That made sense. And so he gave her up until the day he had accumulated enough wealth to maybe own her outright—an exclusivity clause. But that would be a while.

Marnie would edit the shit out of that part, for sure. She'd start with an interrogation about owning women. Then on to the forms of slavery, the forms of prostitution, the difference between them. I thought that I probably write stuff like that just to get it edited. She knows the nature of the dross I'll put in, so that she instinctively knows to take it out.

Robert had come from humble circumstances and saving money toward a goal had been made much clearer to him than, say, the value of any particular life. He had never tortured animals or harmed any person growing up. It just always seemed to him an abstraction that people in movies wept at funerals, an abstraction somehow designed by the moviemakers as a form of hyperbole. Real people didn't carry on like that. They certainly didn't in his family. He thought of his mother as a very efficient element in his life, an element that made it easy for him to be alive, go to school, get from one place to another. He had come to a great appreciation of her. He supposed that's what people meant when they talked about love.

Robert was clearly standing in for a version of Rex at this point, leaving the doc behind. That's the way this business works. If I ever got another interview with Rex we'd go over some of these points, the empathy stuff, the live/dead stuff and how he "felt" about these. I thought I had probably blown my chance with all my inquiries about trained viruses and charging my iPhone. Shit, we never did get back to world peace. Whorled peas. None of it.

The new job was going to be a little complicated. And the complication, as usual, lay in managing the customer's idiosyncratic demands. After being clear about the time element, how that parameter belonged exclusively to Robert, the difficulties began with the client insisting that the death be slow or at least as drawn out as possible. It was amazing to Robert how often he had to deal with this request. The customer wanted the hit to be some kind of medieval draw, peel and quarter: open the body, peel the skin off then dip the still-living victim in saltwater and then pull in four directions with horses. While this exact scenario was not possible, how close could he get to having the victim suffer the maximum amount of pain? Would it cost extra? Well, then paying extra would be no problem. And Robert had to insist that exactly the opposite would be the case if he were hired. The person would be killed as quickly, and, therefore, as painlessly as possible. Short of anaesthetizing the victim first and then administering a lethal cocktail of drugs—sort of an assisted suicide—Robert's form of dispatch would be the next least painless and quickest death. Ah, the gift of death. Why did they always want the long way—he called it the premium-suffering package? Why wasn't death good enough? Dead was dead. Gone was gone. The pain part would just make it ridiculous. And ridiculous death just seemed sad and stupid. And so Robert had to use a number of strategies he'd worked out to turn clients away from the premium package and bring them to the appreciation of what he came to call the "one bee sting" package. One bee sting and then they're gone, returned to the earth as fast as flesh yearned to be dust again. Imagine, he said, that they will simply move from being an immense annoyance in your life to being not there, all in one payment. And you must be satisfied with that very significant fact and forget about all the ways you want to see them squirm before dying. Death is the single and irremediable goal, a goal that really engulfs all others.

Robert thought of death as a cleansing, not in the avenging angel sense, but in the tidying up sense. There was something so elegant and thorough about death. That concept was, finally, what he tried to sell his customer: think of a truly extraordinary house cleaning—windows and everything—and you walk into your house that's fresh and clean to every extremity. That feeling. What's gone is the dirt and confusion of dirt and the way dirt attracts other dirt. Take a deep breath. See how nice that is? You're starting over from an elegant cleanliness. Of course, there will be an accumulation of other dirt over time. But think how long the clean will last. And then maybe you'll learn to live with a little dirt in your life until you need my services again. Clean is a little expensive but certainly worth it. An investment in that exquisitely clean state, even if it can't last forever. Worth every penny. Robert reined in his salesmanship at this point and let the customer ruminate. And mull. And then ponder, consider, etc. There was no hurrying the process. Once, just once, his customer immediately got to his feet and walked out saying, "No, she must suffer. She must suffer until all the nerve endings in her body are . . ." and then out the door.

What is Rex's view of suffering? I know, I think, his view on painting buildings. That feeling of having my head filled as if by cotton candy and words and music all at the same time—I want that again. Writing does it sometimes. The traffic seethed. The traffic stunk and pulsed and then coagulated like old grease.

The mac-and-cheese came hot with pieces of Italian sausage throughout—three cheeses and still bubbling in the casserole. The waitress smiled and said like a big sister, "Hot, hot dish. Very hot." She held up one finger in warning. And then she left.

One person seeking the death of another person seemed to Robert one of the most common occurrences, every day. People wished other people dead but for the most part were willing to live with the other person simply because of the complexity of having the other person killed: the risk of the illegality (of course), the expense, and then the disruption of life. So most wishes were just that, gaseous abstractions left un-acted upon and accumulating like dust balls in the corners of existence. So how much untidiness could one person stand before he hired someone to come in and clean? People had different tolerances. An acquaintance had said that the hardest part of marriage was the first year in which the two parties adjusted their thresholds for untidiness. For a marriage to succeed the clean freak had to come down, the slob come up. Some people seemed to reach the limits of their tolerance quickly and call Robert. Or they simply had the money to clean up and chose to do it. Once you figured out the commonest difficulties in the negotiations and made accommodations or even headed them off before they arrived, the whole enterprise got easier. The suffering part, the particulars of timing, and then there was matter of payment. Most customers had taken from movies some idea of how payment should be made. The contact with the customers would be dragged out endlessly with the "half-now, half-later" cliché from movies. No one in the business did it that way.

Robert began by mentioning payment before the customer could. That way he could state the conditions of payment clearly and directly following the non-negotiable conditions about timing and quickness of death. They came as a package narration. This is how it will be. This is **how it's done by the people who do this sort of thing**. There is no alternative payment schedule, no layaway, no sale price, no amortization. It's a one-time cash transaction whereby you hand me the money, I count it, and we walk away from each other never to be in contact again. You trust that what you paid for will be done properly because you are here making this transaction based on my reputation for keeping a deal sacred. You get what you pay for, but you pay for it first. It will be done. He'd even tried a joke once announcing, "Thy will be done," but the look on the customer's face indicated that Robert had breached the "no-humor" part of the pact. In times of extremis, humor did not lighten the situation; it bred distrust.

So many people came to him already convinced that they would be dealing with a crazy person because only a crazy person would kill other people for a living. And crazy would be fine if only it didn't manifest itself in flippancy (or any other kind of humor) during the negotiated ghoulishness. Robert made the joke just once. And all subsequent negotiations were as monosyllabic and straight-faced as possible. Robert wore gray: a suit and deep green tie without stripes to keep the stimulus as low as possible during negotiations. If the customer believed he was dealing with crazy to get the unthinkable accomplished, he could at least be as comfortable as possible doing it.

The traffic's starting to move a little. You get that traffic thing like a narrative that shoves forward but butts up against something quickly, something you can't see. And that's right where Rex is: do I have the story wrong? What exactly is the story? What's my next move to exhort the story to greater greatness? Rex had escaped the Lucite box and manifested himself as an imperial metaphor colonizing my thinking: fractals, modernism, macaroni-and-cheese, RNA and DNA.

Robert had two glasses of iced tea with the mac-and-cheese: two sugars and squeezed lemon. The waitress asked him how he had liked their special. Robert allowed as it had been as good as advertised.

Robert yawned, the mac-and-cheese concert in his bloodstream singing him to sleep, the iced tea raising a little ruckus to keep him awake. His client had said she'd think about it—all his conditions, she said, all his lecturing. Her eyes darted not side to side like suspicious people, not like lean and hungry Cassius in *Julius Caesar*, but up and down, up and down pathologically. Maybe she had some neurological damage. She had said she'd have to think it over. And generally Robert never took second meetings: for example, she might change her mind and from some moral high horse call the police to make amends and get into heaven. Robert's mother had explained to him that each time it snowed when he was a teenager, there was some old lady who couldn't shovel her walks, and he was to find one for each new snowstorm and shovel her out for free. And then he was sure to get into heaven. Robert liked that his heavenly account book had so many credits, but wondered if the credits held up one to one with the murders or if there was some discount rate. And, alas, every time it snowed, right at the beginning when the first flakes fell, Robert felt a tightening in his gut, and he knew he'd have to shovel one *pro bono* sidewalk. . . . And then he sighed and knew he never had to shovel another walk as long as he lived. But his mother had ruined snow for him.

He pondered whether to take the second meeting with the

lady. No. He didn't need the money even though he really didn't want to be idle either. Like everything else there was a season to his business. He had met a surgeon at an event once and the surgeon said there was clearly a seasonal component to his work. Christmas season was especially busy for elective surgery. January and February were busy for Robert. He thought the phenomenon could be explained by the post-holidays-blues syndrome reported in all newspapers, the letdown and melancholy of January, the high suicide rates of February. Leaden skies. Leaden souls. And in some people the blues begat rage and rage always looked for some place to attach itself. Rage alone was mere unhappiness. Rage *at* something, someone—now that felt like something.

How old would a person have to be before rage went away? Robert had encountered Dylan Thomas's poem, "Do Not Go Gentle into that Good Night," but "rage, rage against the dying of the light." What old person had the energy left? The poem was about a young man thinking about what it was like for an old man to die. But it was the young man's rage. Robert had always found in poetry a convenient compendium of human emotions, a kind of encyclopedia of what he supposed were legitimate human responses. The legitimacy came, Robert deduced, through the fact that the poem had been first published and then anthologized. And those two things could only happen if a number of people agreed that the poem really did capture what it was to be a human being. To Robert, many of the findings in the poems seemed like abstractions: the sacredness of human life, grief over the loss of a loved one, absence as a powerful wrenching of the human psyche, love or yearning after that distorted reality—it all seemed so inconvenient, but Robert knew that if he didn't try to understand this business, he would not be able to plan his murders.

Ah, Rex. Wherefore art thou in this thing of love? I'd be willing to listen long and hard to your disquisition on the subject. I'd sit quietly, hands on my knees. Rapt. You could tell me about love and I would interrogate the universe on the subject. Okay. Maybe that's getting away from me.

For a short time, Robert thought of his end product as "eliminations," ridding the world of another competing hunger for scarce supplies—a kind of Malthusian scourge. But very quickly he returned to the actual word *murder*, as the best and least deceptive. The way to succeed in his business, Robert figured, was to deceive oneself as little as possible, cut though the dross to the actual while others—police, revenge seekers—were running around in worlds of illusion and fraudulent surfaces and misdirection trying to find the hand in the sleight-of-hand.

After a walk along the river to settle the mac-and-cheese, he decided: he would not see the woman again unless she called to present a valid case for not hiring him during the first encounter. Lack of funds for the payoff would be valid. Maybe the victim really didn't deserve to die, would not be valid.

Once some years ago, Robert had received an urgent message after the payment had been made, the deal consummated. The message said he could keep half the money but shouldn't carry out the killing. The client had changed his mind. Robert thought: changed his mind about what? Robert laughed to himself. Maybe I should just wing the hit, like in the cowboy movies. Shoot the victim in the hand, and then send back half the money. Or maybe I should just fire a couple warning shots in the air. Or, no, even better, I should catch the victim unawares and give him a good, hard slap in the face. Followed by a good talking-to. Followed by . . .

He shot the contracted-for man directly in the side of the head—a bee sting as clean as the wrath of God. And just as ineffable. A deal was a deal.

This version of a Rex-world had already occurred to me. And it had certainly occurred to Dr. S. The last meeting in his new digs—new lab coat not withstanding—Dr. S had exhibited a vague uneasiness over what Rex was up to, might get up to eventually and the nothing he was able to do about it. Dr. S has seemed sideways with his creation and maybe even with creation itself. The traffic seemed to burp and pass gas all at once. And begin to move.

The woman had left messages in the designated manner. She wanted to meet again. Why? he asked her, by the same message post. She had all the money now, she said. And Robert allowed as she had given the correct response to earn a second meeting.

Robert watched her at the café table for a half hour. He noted all the people on the street, who passed by, who lingered, if any came back again, if any changed clothes and came back to loiter. One elderly man went in and out of a shop, stopped on the sidewalk, looked in the window, went in again, came out again. Finally, Robert decided that he was the one, whether the accidental dithering of an old man or the police officer designated to arrest him, it didn't matter. He was the anomaly that blew the deal. It only took one. Robert felt quite accomplished leaving the woman the message that declared the null and the void. No business. Goodbye.

Robert thought that being more careful than anyone else could even conceive would allow him to retire someday. He had even thought about what he could do in retirement: he would move to a small town and become an exterminator of unwanted pests: skunks under the house, raccoons raiding fishponds, squirrels in the attic, a bee swarm on the front porch. "What's the difference?" he thought. He would just take on interesting jobs when he felt like it, jobs that made the community a better place to live. And he would read poetry and discover the human condition. Pretty soon now he would have enough.

Ah, now this one might be interesting. Robert found a park bench and cracked open the newspaper. Partners in an art gallery had come to public blows over how each thought the other had skimmed funds and . . . oh, here was a better one yet. Two brothers, longtime partners in land deals all over the world, had gone to court to disentangle their finances and go their separate ways. Both men had found the judgment unacceptable and unfair. Robert thought, wouldn't that be the indication that the judgment really worked? Both parties aggrieved equally? But no, the brothers planned to tie up the separation in complex, global-financing ways to keep the other from getting on with his financial life. Perfect, thought Robert. He'd flip a coin to decide which brother to contact.

But before he began negotiations, Robert thought he might have one more round of that mac-and-cheese.

Rex not eating anything, apparently, might have set off the whole mac-and-cheese thing. Rex as judge and jury eventually set off another part. Rex's choice of colors for the trucking company made these first two all the more frightening. Bad boy, Rex. Bad boy.

The coroner found that the Italian sausage cured for six weeks hanging in a humidity controlled room to grow the proper mold covering—one batch of that sausage had somehow been infected by a rogue pathogen when the electricity had failed briefly. The pathogen had been isolated; it shouldn't have been there in the sausage cure. It was found dead but apparently had been alive for a short time in the sausages. Attempts to identify it had included microbiologists from a nearby university who declared it "new and deadly toxic." Their report had indicated that the toxin it produced might leave in a victim the equivalent signature of a heart attack. But a quick bloom of the pathogen would certainly be deadly in certain individuals with European DNA. It seemed less toxic in Asian or African DNA. It seemed the "new" pathogen was a single accident of mutation—short lived and deadly, but found nowhere else.

The sausage maker had lost his food license until authorities could make sure that his particular "old world" process didn't contribute to the mutation. There was only one known death from the tainted sausage: Robert Neff found slumped on a park bench along the river esplanade.

Miraculously the traffic broke as if a plug had been pulled and let the carbon-consumers roll on their various ways across the city—to love, to loneliness, the suffering and joy.

Chapter VI

Marnie and I tried to shake off our hectic week by going out to dinner (no movie), getting a couple bottles of wine and just drinking and talking the night away. Forget Dr. S, forget fractal art and the slurp of white wine while standing up in the gallery. We started with phones off, a fine layer of meal with the first bottle, and then the second bottle was for on top, for the laughing and forgetting the crazy week. I hadn't told her about speaking to Rex. I knew I would have to sometime, but I had to be sure what the "speaking" part actually was. Did Dr. S arrange the whole thing like the Wizard of Oz from behind a curtain? As I said, even that version was a great twist on the mad-scientist story, a potential article more interesting than DNA, mitochondria, broken genetic material. The talking bowl of oatmeal wouldn't fly by itself—too much ground work and backstory before an editor would even countenance it. But a wacked-out scientist with an elaborate puppet show, that was immediately great stuff if we got to look behind the curtain. Problem was, I still couldn't find the curtain.

Marnie was celebrating lots of sales of the fractals. The artist in each case was actually a collaboration of mathematician and designer or color person who decided on color values. One set of prints came from a Japanese mathematician who made his own color schemes. All the rest were collaborations. And each collaboration had its own deal or split of the profit. In some cases, the mathematician got the lion's share because the cunning reiteration of the polynomial was deemed by the cooperating pair as the most important part—the ground work, the RNA set of instructions. In other cases, the color schemes or values assigned within the formula was understood to be the key. Marnie told me she had spreadsheets for the complicated deals each artist-pair set up. Sometimes, she said, the split changed with the size of the canvas or reproduction. She couldn't figure out exactly why, but apparently the collaborators knew.

This whole collaborative business in art had a National Science Foundation ring to it. Dr. S worked in a barn with a Lucite box and a bowl of oatmeal until he hit the collaborative jackpot with the NSF. Or some great money sump, anyway, that emptied out into his suite of offices. My first inclination is to suspect the military that has endless funds to throw at projects of potential strategic value. What kind of killing advantage would Rex give them? Could Rex blow shit up? Would he make a good soldier? If, like a fractal, any part of him was exactly like the whole of him, wouldn't that make generating a gazillion of him a mere button-push away? Talk about hearing voices! The perversely inquiring part of me, the apocalypse-curious part, would love to be seated in the front row right after that button push. Blah, blah, blah indeed.

At dinner, one bottle gone, the next on its way, we toasted life's crazy fullness.

"To life's crazy fullness," I proposed. We drank what was left in our glasses.

"To how heartbreakingly beautiful life is sometimes," Marnie toasted after the next bottle arrived. "Maybe we should drink to that in pieces," she added. "You know, first to heartbreaking beauty, then to . . . what?"

"To sometimes," I tried. She liked that, and we drank to sometimes.

We had a game we played in which we'd answer each other as different literary characters (or artists, she insisted, so we put that in) during regular conversation. She'd do Anna Karenina on the subject of dinner guests for next weekend.

"They all know, of course. Except the countess. She doesn't know anything."

"Ever?"

"Ever! But the others, they all know and talk behind my back."

Understand that this was well into the second bottle. At the end of the bottle, I felt I had to tell Marnie that I'd been speaking to Rex, and now he'd fallen silent—sort of. I should have either explained the jump better or prepared her for my confession because she thought we were still in the game. Maybe we were.

"So . . ." The pause, as I look back, was supposed to be the signal that we'd changed out of the game. Maybe it wasn't long enough.

"So . . ." I said. "This guy I've been interviewing, the DNA experimenter guy. Anyway, he let me talk to his experiment—not the last time but the time before. The last time Rex wouldn't talk at all. . . . Wait. Let me back up."

Without a hitch Marnie began to do an impression of Georgia O'Keefe. She did an Irish-Hungarian Wisconsin dairy farmer accent that is difficult to replicate because the wine brought in a few more eastern European nuances with an occasional Swede in the low spots. Marnie is a very funny woman. Then she soared. I waited it out until she began cracking herself up and the neighboring tables began to look over at us in unison. I should have saved Rex for another time but, alas, didn't, and continued after Marnie had done her thing.

"So . . ." I said, "I was talking to him about his work, and he asked me if I'd like to speak directly to Rex. I had met Rex before, you know, the couple of early interviews. Well, met in the sense that I saw him there in the corner, sulking, I thought."

"And how did you know he vas a he?" Still half transformed into the Irish-Hungarian, but coming around.

"I was assuming from the name, and then Dr. S always used the male pronoun referring to goo in the corner. So I said, sure, I'd like to talk to Rex as directly as possible." Then I told her about the computer version, then—pause—finally, the sense that Rex was inside my head, like having earbuds on. But no earbuds, I think. Maybe the doctor had some way of doing this, some form of stunt he was pulling."

"You're serious? The blob talked in your head?" She laughed. I don't think she laughed at me, but at the talking blob image she'd made.

"That's right. I played along, you know, just to see where it would go. And the more I sort of consented to the whole charade, the more reasonable it became. Does that make any sense?"

She returned to her heaviest accent, whatever it was, to demonstrate that, of course, this is exactly what we've been talking about with the game *we* played. The longer the better.

"And I talked to Rex about this whole being-and-becoming business. Again, sort of. And he let me know that we, humans that is, wouldn't like it if he changed things into what we think they should be. He implied our ideals were impractical. No, maybe just false or unrealistic. That if we were changed into what was necessary for everything to be ideal—you, know, peace, justice, kindness, that stuff—then he'd have to do away with the way we are." It was coming out tangled in the wine, the game, and Marnie's beautiful eyes that were getting wider and wider.

"Wine or not, you've gotta be shitting me," she said with some flourish. "Dr. Seuss has you believing that the blob talks to you inside your head. Number one. And number deux, the blob is a combination of Wittgenstein and Kierkegaard. Care to add Hunter S. Thompson?"

I loved the way she laughed at her own jokes, a chuckle starting low and then overtaking her and shaking her whole body. It made funny even funnier. More wine.

She continued when she got the laughing stopped. "And . . . and what's it like when the blob's in your head?"

"Rex."

"Okay, Rex. Is it like God talking to you? Like being possessed?"

"Like wearing earbuds. Like Pandora. Like those announcements in train stations that come on and seem to come from everywhere at once. Maybe he'd talk to you too. Wanna come along some time? He'd like you, I think. But then there's the whole shutting up thing. He seems to have shut up in his new digs. And speaking of new digs—"

"So Rex has taken some kind of vow of silence?" She started to giggle again. "Who would he be vowing to? Now *that* seems like an interesting question. The disembodied head takes a monk's vow, except . . . except . . ."

She can't keep it in anymore and has to talk through the giggles.

"Except . . ." She holds up one hand to stop herself from laughing. Wine.

"Okay, okay." Big breath. "Except that it's like an identity thing, his vow. He has to vow to . . . to . . ." Not again. "To his algorithm. No, to his agar-agar. No, to his zeroes and to his—"

"Yeah, ones." I may as well get in here. But I'm so pleased by her giggle-fest that I can't get annoyed by her self-indulgent silliness. "On the other hand," I begin, to change directions slightly. "What kind of religious experience must *I* be having. Huh? Huh? I mean having direct contact with the beginning of the end? With the messianic oatmeal blob goo? How cool is that? I think you should get in on this as soon as possible. I don't want to be the only one besides the doctor who can hear this voice. Can't really tape record the inside of my own head. Since I love you so much I'm sure you'll be included in a package deal with me."

"Speak, Rex! Speak!" She says. And more wine. I think she's the funniest person on earth. So, at this moment, does she.

* * *

Marnie's off to work early. I'm lagging into breakfast bit by bit, caffeine first. The Tuesday *New York Times* is open on the table and beginning to draw me into the world. And like my friend's bus-plunge notations, there they are: action-at-a-distance, remote control, matter being mind-moved. The times they are a-changing.

Item: Amazonian expedition comes back with a ground plant that takes up heavy metals from the soil and renders them into unstable proteins that break down in soil to provide fertilizer.

Item: Three new fungi discovered that live on clean glass, eating nothing but silicon in the glass itself. All glass forms apparently can be metabolized by the new species. Some discussion about adding a new phylum. Phylogeneticists on alert. New branch of fungi.

Item: (And here I'm working with the direction already provided by the first two, but I'm susceptible, suggestion prone.) Child born without sinus cavities in Brazil has grown older and now displays an ability to, instead of smell, somehow intuit odors through some combination of visual and tactile clues. He says he "knows" odors in the context of his constant headaches.

Item: Local invasive species, teasel (*dipsacus*), has displayed carnivorous characteristics, consuming insects that get caught in rainwater deposits that accumulate along its stem. While not a new observation, the teasel observed has formed hard spikes in the seedpods that have begun to display some of the characteristics of alloys of metals.

And finally, item: Local high school football star renounces football and tries to get his teammates to quit, too. Claims head injury suffered early in the season has given him visions as to "how humans must conduct themselves" in this life, and football is the wrong direction.

More caffeine and the pattern emerged, the pattern I was prepared for, anyway. Rex was out there and adjusting the world.

I made an appointment with Joan to see Dr. S again. She said it would have to be three weeks out since he was busy conducting a conference at the university, a conference on AI and allied arts. That's what she said, "allied arts." So I asked her what were some of the allied arts, and she said she wasn't certain, but that some formidable scholars (her word, "formidable") were expected for the conference. The registration fee for attending the conference was $1,200 a pop. She said they wanted to limit attendance but that the university students were all allowed in free with a university ID card.

Good enough, I thought. Fake IDs were not going to be a problem. Let's see what's cooking. Maybe Rex will give his first public performance.

I paid $75 for a fake student ID—the going rate, I was told. A second-class felony they also said, class C maybe. My contact just wanted me to know the risks and that I would never find him again. That was the deal—a good-enough ID, seventy-five bucks, and mum's the word.

Marnie said she was unsure whether she wanted to be an accessory to any felony, much less ones after B in the alphabet. C, D, E, F and G felonies, she reasoned must have nastier punishments, the farther they got away from the grade A: grade A eggs, grade A on the essay. Grade A nimrod, I suggested. Finally, she relented and gave me a makeover designed to reduce my thirty-something years to twenty-something. When she got done with the makeup brushes, the hair trim (she said she made it look longer by cutting it—*mirabile dictu, mirabile visu*) and the nose hair trimming (twenties don't have nose hair problems, she claimed), I was ready. The clothing concoction she came up with, I claimed, made her thoroughly complicit and an accessory before the fact, *ipse dixit*. The Latin stuff she was just showing off. She contended that I would have a better chance passing if I threw around a little Latin once in a while. Then the laugh again. How would I live without her after Rex declared the apocalypse and handed the world over to cockroaches and ants?

The attendance at the conference was an exclusive club of scientists who, I suspected, had even nicer lab coats than Dr. S and then add a minor infection of science students and then me undercover. Here's how that worked:

Dr. S, at the first plenary session, sees me come in and says, "Oh, it's you. How've you been?" Busted. But no matter. He wasn't interested in the revenue from the conference fees.

"Has Rex asked about me?" I thought I'd try Dr. Seuss mode without the rhymes. "Does he still talk to you? Is he here today?"

The good doctor cocked his head at me, looked over my shoulder, said, "Excuse me, I have to talk to someone over there," and scurried off.

I found a place to sit on the aisle so I could stretch out, got ready my notebook, pricked up my ears.

Dr. S began with a eulogy, and I use the term I think precisely: a eulogy for Rex, the recently departed. No more the sentient blob, the striped conjurer, hunkered in the corner of his Lucite realm. No more wizardry of speaking over someone's neurons with or without permission. Dr. S droned.

"Rex was an experiment in a particular set of recursive algorithms. He was, in a way, a closed system." (No mention, I should note, about speaking the King's English to freaked-out journalists.) "A system of instructions to eat—okay (creaky laugh), and then go forth and multiply. The limits of his—its, hers, theirs, the alternatives are present in the discussion—his limits were heat, light, food . . . and, I suppose, my good will. His limits were also the original set of instructions."

I'm thinking, that sounds like humans—the original set of instructions have all this built-in "shit happens" and that's the story of the whole breed. Tragedy, evil, sadness and despair . . .

The drone seemed to have left Dr. S's voice: he strengthens. He grows. "Rex was a prototype for AI, I suppose. But the 'I' part was a sliding scale from the beginning. We're all here to negotiate that scale today. When does intelligence kick in? Plants are full of cunning—slime molds and fungi to complex replication in aspen groves cloning themselves. Does that count as intelligence? Weather patterns have contingent structures that think out—sort of—their relationship to each other and then react—sort of—to complex stimuli—sort of—and alter themselves in response. . . . Yes, sort of all the way. So it was with Rex."

I heard here echoes of the funeral oration Marc Anthony gives for Caesar.

The doctor's voice had attained a mellow deepness reminiscent of Orson Welles, the later years. Where did that baritone come from? He continued, backing away from the microphone a precise distance, like a pro, the distance that made the sound system in perfect sympathy. He voice-licked the entire audience.

"Rex died ten days ago of some kind of internal clock that I must have included in the program, though I didn't build in anything on purpose. He grew old and died. A form of intelligence—and here I reluctantly leave out 'sort of'—came and went. Sentience? Causality? Perspicacity and cunning and purpose? Yes, purpose. All these we've come here today to debate. The discursive nature of intelligence is an invitation to discourse—that's the tautology. And, finally, the teleology too. What does this business of AI include? What ultimate causes and effects and reasons and . . . here's the word again, sympathies?"

This was great stuff: stentorian tones, invocations of duty and purpose, challenges to human intelligence. And then, after a slight pause, the doctor's direction shifted.

"Are we willing to move over? If we find a newer, better, more responsive intelligence—if we create this intelligence or if we find it—are we willing to graciously acknowledge its superiority and move over? I challenge you here today to ask yourself this question: if I can plainly see the next step higher in intelligence, am I willing to hand over the keys to the kingdom? Am I willing to forego jealousies and petty species-ist favoritisms to the great, higher, more clearly god-like good? Could I live in peace with a higher intelligence that would supply me food, shelter, beautiful vistas, the time to make art and breed? Would I allow myself to be kept like a pet? Warmed and cooled, my food dish kept full?"

Jesus, I thought. General Buck Turgidson's speech in the War Room in the movie *Dr. Strangelove* where he reads the wacky note from Brigadier General Jack D. Ripper. Or maybe the cuckoo comes out, the cross-eyed cuckoo comes out of a clock and everyone knows that madness is the order of the day. I looked around at the audience. Not a buzz, not a sideways glance of discomfort. They were spellbound and the microphone was the wizard's wand.

Pregnant pause from the doctor. Then, "Well, are you? Are you willing to go quietly to a superior plane in the name of greater intelligence, a more thoroughly reasonable world? It's been in the cards for a long time. It's been coming and coming since we could first imagine the better version of this slag heap world of anger and greed and small-minded pettiness. Would you say yes? What Thomas Carlyle called the 'Everlasting Yea,' would you assent? What if I told you that I knew where you could find this intelligence? You could run your biological, your ethical, your philosophical tests on it. It would submit to any interrogation, any investigation of motives ulterior, interior, theoretical. It would calm your fears, be patient with all probing and finally hold your hand while you sighed and . . . what? Capitulated? Began to worship? God and gods have always met with resistance when they manifested themselves. And the stories of these resistances have always come from humans who were certain they would resist out of pure mud-born stubbornness and refusal to recognize that God had come."

Now I was sure there would be stirrings in the audience and harrumphing in general, and the white coats and looney nets would come out to get the doc. But no. It was only me who was immune to the charms of his speech, it seemed. Only me unlicked by the voice coming from the dais.

The doctor hitched up his rhetoric. "I am come to tell you today, he is here." The pause was so long after this statement that only the slight buzz of the PA system sang on into the gathering seconds, a minute? Probably not quite. Dr. S broke the silence. "The new time is begun. The new set of values and goals is here. The only immediate problem is that . . . humans are in the way."

Damn, I thought. Maybe these guys talk to each other this way all the time, and I'm the only one who thinks the inmates have taken over the home for the bewildered. Was the ubiquitous bottled water at the conference really Kool-Aid? The audience didn't seem to know quite what to do as Dr. S indicated he was finished. They applauded, at first politely, then more and more in a crescendo that made me think once more of drinking the Kool-Aid. What a flavorful lunacy this was. High-powered men and women of the AI world from business to universities where they hide out, are come together to begin the world anew. The article was writing itself. Rhetorical questions: Who will resist a better and more intelligent world? Who will hold back humanity in the name of all the patent ugliness and inhumanity of humans to other humans? Who will deny the new gods their due? Who will sigh and long for the old days of poverty and pain? (Punchier—they should be punchier.) What rough beast, its hour come round at last, slouches toward Bethlehem to be born? (Mr. Yeats, of course, but it's such a great line—talk about punchy). How about these? New gods, new world. Egad, new gods (kind of works). And then maybe . . . new masters but no slaves.

I scribbled on and on in my notebook. The applause thinned and finally died. What did they expect? An encore? Doctor Sewall, Dr. Seuss, still at the dais, waited and then walked slowly into the wings. Had I just heard him declaring the revelation, make that the Revelation, that begins the end? Spores. Something Dr. S had reported earlier about spores being Rex going for a walk outside the AG barn. And then the news items as if new life forms were being tried out in fits and starts, Rex harmlessly playing at sprites, dryads and faeries. And somehow in the fuzzy recesses of this whole business, fractals. What was it about fractals? Were fractals the answer or the question? The reiterations? The litany?

During a break, I asked an older gentleman from a prestigious West Coast university what he thought of Dr. Sewall's opening remarks. He smiled and explained to me with great patience that he took the speech to be something like an invitation to debate certain ideas. That the speech simply jumped, without explanation, to a state of investigation of AI sometime in the future when that same exact speech would be made seriously.

A-ha! I thought. I wonder if everybody thought that Dr. S had been in a sort of ironic antagonist mode during the speech. I asked around at the table that held the small Danish pastries and coffee. The next version (from a younger professor, Midwestern university bastion of AI investigation partially funded by Intel) was that we were, or had been, in the presence of a kind of comic book version of the enterprise of AI, the look-out-here-they-come version, the *I Robot* fear mongering of older generations that really did no credit to the intellectual discipline. But, that said, he continued, Doctor Sewall had paid for all the best thinkers to get together for a couple days and talk to each other. No NSF money, apparently, and therefore no elaborate reporting back on how the money was spent. Here he indicated the pastries and the urns of Starbucks coffee. And each attendant did not have to solicit his or her own university for travel funds. An all-expenses-paid junket to chew the fat with our best intellectual friends, some of whom we have only known through scientific papers—who could say no? So all was forgiven if the opening convocation was high-riding rhetoric and comic incursions.

Really? Wow. That put the whole thing in perspective. I wanted to (but didn't) tell the young gentleman scientist about visiting Rex in his original lair, about having my neurons appropriated for a sound system, about the change in Dr. S's voice and demeanor and venue and lab coat—the lab coat syndrome! I thought he might like to know about the stripes Rex sported in Rex Prime stage, about the plain snarkiness of the crabby child-

Rex when he ran out of agar-agar or fructose or whatever the hell he was eating at the time. And, of course, there was the post-Rex interview intellectual buzz I experienced in the land of fractals and cheap white wine and elbow patches.

I realized I didn't really have much in the way of evidence, just hints and inklings and surreal, non-verifiable experiences reported by a person (me) who got paid to see the unseen, wow a jaded reading audience, and make his living in the realm of creative nonfiction: emphasis on creative. The Assembler. I wasn't ready to sing that song in public much less to a group of experts whose job it was to be skeptical and roll their eyes at the fantastic versions of the deadly serious life work they pursued.

Who was getting off on the speech something like I was?—the students. There was a cluster of them in the corner identifiable by the skinny jeans and bad haircuts. Two of them were riffing on the speech to three others. The two were doing their best version of SNL or maybe Ken Jennings welcoming "our new masters" at the end of the *Jeopardy* loss to the IBM computer, Watson. They apparently thought the speech was hilarious parody and that Dr. S was a comic genius. The "death of Rex" part was played by a young man who spoke as oatmeal would speak. Another said he was moved to capitulate immediately if there would be sex and barbecue in "heaven." I moved on.

Dr. S was surrounded by colleagues. He seemed taller, his skin a better color, his back straighter, his voice deeper. He spoke easily with his colleagues, basking in the ebb and the flow of admiration—for the amenities of the conference? For the speech? I couldn't tell. He glowed.

It was a while before I could get an interview with Dr. Sewall himself. He was at first surrounded by admirers eager to enter the discursive doors he'd opened with his speech. Students gathered in worship groups, scattered and then reformed like Vaux Swifts in an evening sky. Quickly the break was over and the groups broke up into rooms for the various sessions with titles like: "AI, Poor Stepchild or Aging Grandfather." And my favorite: "After Intelligence—Whence the Post-Intelligence Apocalypse?"

And so Dr. S wasn't actually available until lunch break—but I had no chance as he schmoozed off with other dignitaries. Then toward the afternoon, my vigilance in the hallways paid off as he slipped out of a session that had apparently gone south of stimulating, and then furtively tried sneaking off down the hallway toward where the afternoon hosted bar was being set up. Free booze—the guy knew how to run a conference.

"Dr. Sewall. Could I have a minute?" He held up two fingers to the student bartender and two vodka tonics appeared with a minimum of glass clinking. He handed me one.

"I see your interest in theoretical intelligence forms hasn't waned, Mr. James."

"Jacob," I went formal for the serious vibe. ."I found your speech fascinating, your opening remarks."

"Some of my less imaginative colleagues found some signs of incipient madness in my welcome. Others, not so bad. So, maybe a wash. Thought it was worth taking a chance. What did you think? A journalist's opinion please."

Something in the straight back, the good skin, the self-possession, like he'd gone to Norman Vincent Peale school or at least done the correspondence course or maybe just a skin peel. "I . . . I found . . . I thought . . . I *detected* something of Marc Anthony's funeral oration for Julius Caesar in your words on the passing of Rex. Do you miss him?"

He swirled the drink. "Well, I really just made heat and light and food available for him. Really more like keeping a goldfish. There wasn't a great bond, you know. Not like having a golden retriever." His laugh, something about the laugh.

"But you wrote the code that he was. That was something."

"Zeroes and ones. Ones and zeroes, Jake. And do you 'miss' him? After all, he seemed to take to you. He never really talked to anyone else after you. I don't know why."

"Was it a conjurer's trick, the whole talking business?"

"You tell me, Mr. Investigative Reporter." And then the laugh. Something new with the old tee-hee of the goofy professor missing. This laugh, this world-weary existential angst laugh, this . . . I found myself writing the article as we spoke and casting about for what I would do with the laugh. As if Albert Camus had appeared in an old John Wayne movie, but sitting back with his feet up against the general store railing and laughing about the horse-opera negotiations going on in front of him. Jesus, no! But some kind of odd juxtaposition of maybe *Leave It to Beaver* and Jean Genet's *The Maids*. I'd never actually turned that in to an editor either. I was circling the laugh, though.

The doctor continued. "Do you think Rex was a worthwhile experiment?"

"I have to admit I was . . . am still trying to process the talking part."

"It's not really that hard, you know. You were thinking about whether the thing was alive and also how you'd interview it if it really was. I could tell—like right now—you are always writing even when you're trying to get material from someone. So that writing voice in your head—I'd look there first for the Rex voice."

Not so fast. I knew what I knew about that voice and was not about to be talked out of it too quickly. I would cop to temporary insanity first. I could tell my writing voice in my head from the Rex voice. "So Rex is actually gone, or just decommissioned?" But I remember, about age fifteen, when I couldn't tell the voices from the world. Hormones made the bridge, apparently. And the whole confusing year and half was over quickly, though during its height, I also remember how completely wonderful it was to have the inside of my head thoroughly resonant with the outside world, how seamlessly the testosterone boiling in my blood also seared the world. A leaf brushing my face was the world making love to me. I learned, also, to keep my own observations to sullen grunts and incomprehensible vowel sounds. It worked out better that way. But the heat in my blood . . . and then the rich cacophony of voices curling and swirling around each other. And then it was over.

Dr. S set down his empty drink and signaled for another. I indicated I was fine by covering up my glass. He continued, "Interesting question, I think. Decommissioned . . . or gone? On some level, those would be the same thing, of course. Back into constituent piles of ingredients. Sort of a reverse recipe, you might say. But if you think of Rex as a series of instructions—a peculiarly *successful* series of instructions. Because nobody else seems to have . . . Not exactly, anyway. Just wait a minute. Some of my colleagues have done some engaging concocting themselves . . ."

"But no Rex's. No bride of Franken—"

"—No. NO! We try never to use that word in my world."

The second "no" was, it occurred to me, way out of proportion in loudness to the rest of the conversation. Like a child's foot-stomping protest. Like mentioning *Macbeth* in a theater greenroom.

Calmed, the doctor continued after a good slug of his drink. One more of those, I thought, and we'd have vodka talking, and I knew from experience that sometimes that made great interview material. "So, Jake, as I said, Rex, a set of instructions—okay, and a little proprietary magic—was a transition figure in the world of AI. My colleagues had largely been thinking in terms of machines and code and self-improving programs, and complexity. Not many of us were thinking: simple, organic, replications, gender, related genus, you know, the meat route. Turned out Rex was not meat, though. Well, you saw, didn't you? Rex was a timely accident who looked something like porridge. You have to admit that he was impressive at first and then quickly, I think, not very interesting."

"Oh, I can tell you that the talking part was interesting, no matter what kind of self-delusion you suggest. In any case, it was very engaging to hallucinate in the presence of a doctor and his creation, and have the whole thing confirmed."

"Alas, no longer with us." He looked at his expensive watch as if he had to be somewhere else.

"And how did you terminate Rex? Do you say terminate? Pull the plug? Return the ingredients to the shelf?" (I was writing out loud, again.)

"To tell the truth, and I largely *do* tell the truth these days, you may have noticed, Rex is not really terminated or gone in the sense you mean. I think you mean dead. Maybe inorganic? In any case, I think it would be prudent to put it something like . . . Rex is reabsorbed into life—not without life—just indistinguishable now from life itself, in general. Does that make sense? Oh look, here they come from the last session. Meet-and-greet time. Have a wonderful time at our conference, Jake. Your student badge should work for everything, but if you have any problems, just let me know and I'll see you get a press pass. You might have done that from the beginning."

And he was subsumed into the admiring crowd beginning to slurp up lubricating liquor loudly. I backed off to the interstitial buzz by the door then, and finally, after getting an overall view of the mob of theoretical acumen, I slunk away.

Chapter VII

Doctor Sewall had changed and kept changing like a flower blooming. He held sway; he was the bold expression. He manifested himself in ever more fruitful ways. He was like Ralph Waldo Emerson's "great and crescive self"—the 19th century ideal for American Romanticism. I was trying out all this for the article, the article, by the way, that I still had no idea where it was headed. I started out in one direction with Rex-the-cute as center. Moving on then to the slaughter-of-the-innocents new center with Rex blasting over the human consciousness like the PA system in *Brave New World.*

At the beginning of my journalism-for-money career, I had a tendency to get interested in my topics and then wander off into self-indulgent research that was going no place in particular. I ended up with articles that were the parings of stacks of research and compilations of endless hours I chased around in a particular topic—chased my tail it turned out. I met a journalist who did only what was necessary for each article—interviews, research, background—and made three times the money I was making. I was having my own kind of fun to get a living, I suppose, by straying constantly from the point. So I self-corrected and got better and better at, as they say in grade school, staying on task. The voices would seem irrelevant here, but they weren't. I recognized fairly early on that some of the voices were showing me the stuff that was off task, the ever-branching subjects that led me further and further afield from . . . the task. I also realized, but not so quickly, that the task itself was negotiable. Someone else was supplying the task while the voices were jolly and irrational in directing me to anything else, everything else.

But this Dr. S business had me back into old habits. First, I wanted to chase down the whole intellectual hybrid of computers and DNA replication. Then, there was the cult of personality: Dr.

S's apotheosis to the head of the class, the scholars' internecine jealousies and backbiting as reputations rose and fell with finer and finer distinctions in the disciplines. The pecking order. The ladder up and who was standing on whose shoulders. What Nobel Prize was slowly descending from the clouds and choosing one aspirant for immortality. Then there was also the comedy of Rex the cosmic goof. That's a Jack Kerouac term, if I remember right. The cosmic goof that consumes all high seriousness into the True. Dharma meets karma meets Abbott and Costello. Rex as high comedian was the real story I wanted to pursue, but also the hardest to write and damned hard to sell no matter how entertaining I made it. I knew that the best shot at a sale was what I came to call, "It's alive!" Man makes critter and amazes the scientific and philosophical world. Period. Skip the hijinks.

Marnie to the rescue—at first. She helps me redirect and focus. She talks me out of the cosmic goof scenario (though privately I harbor a lingering fondness for this dead end), and then she declares that she wants to come with me to meet Dr. S.

Thinking back on this meeting, I wonder about the whole subject of volition. Did she actually want to meet him or did he decide he wanted to meet her? I mentioned her to him a couple times in our various conversations, so her existence was known to Dr. S, to Dr. S and his new partner, as I think of it now.

Anyway, the meeting: I took her along to the debriefing session about the conference—what got accomplished, what's new, what's shaking in general. And instead of being met by his beautiful assistant, Dr. S himself comes out of his inner sanctum all ablaze in his fresh doctor coat with its intricate stitching that identifies his scientific pedigrees and his new grant money: National Institute of Mental Health (NIMH) and National Science Foundation (NSF) and wherever he got the conference money . . . *But wait, there's more.* I immediately think of this phrase from late-night TV ads as Dr. S appears. The more is a kind of glow by now as if someone had completed the makeover and then polished up the results and then repackaged . . . Wait, there's more. The doctor has cheekbones and done something to his hair that makes it look like a $400 haircut. The slump is completely gone, the skin tight, the teeth whiter, the gut flatter, and . . . he's taller. Worse yet, he ignores me and begins to charm the undies off Marnie, never letting his gaze flag, seeming to caress her with laughs and wit and voice-licks. I stand by helplessly watching this guy seduce my girl. I try to get a word in, start the interview, and Dr. S reaches over and lays his hand gently on my shoulder while he prattles on to Marnie, and I swear I stood there paralyzed by his touch. I was a fish caught in the jellyfish tentacle. I tried to speak, tried to walk out of the gentle grip on my shoulder. I couldn't. I listened while he got her babbling about her art world, then shot her a few references to get her to expand on her art knowledge, then. . . . Well, the entire seduction symphony, all the instruments from the flute trills to the big basses filling the soundscape with sexy growls and far away roars. French horns. Violas. Banks of violins.

Finally, after he'd made his music run up and down her spinal cord, after he'd twanged a while on her central nervous system, he took his hand off my shoulder and I could talk again. I stumbled into the interview after separating him from Marnie, got my information, all the while feeling I had just yanked Juliette away from Romeo and kicked her down the stairs. As we left, again his gaze lapped her face like a lab puppy does a stick of butter. Outside his office Marnie seemed in a trance of some sort. I guessed she hadn't been so thoroughly chatted up and courted since I plied her with my proletarian version, lo those years ago. But Dr. S did a pro job, I admitted. All the moves, nothing left out.

She said later that she "liked him." And that all I had told her about the schlumpy mad-scientist didn't seem to fit the real guy.

"Of course you 'liked him,'" I whined. "He did everything but lay you down and give you a full oil-up body massage and then stuff hundred dollar bills in your panties." I could hear my whine but couldn't stop myself. I could see her eyes narrowing at my icky jealousy but couldn't stop myself. I was taken over by my own unpleasantness. So I went on. "Couldn't you see what he was trying to do? Couldn't you? *Why are women so . . .*" And here I knew I was blowing it big time. Never begin an inquiry with these four words. There is nowhere to go, no possible language that could follow these four. No logical sequence possible that will get you out of it. And yet I heard myself continue as she took a step back, narrowed her eyes, crossed her arms over her breasts—all the contraindications like an ordered set in mathematics that lead in only one direction. I said, ". . . so, prone, so unaware, so apt"—oh, I was digging the hole—"so insensate to blither, the blather, the insincere . . ." I should have fallen silent, defeated by language, but I was driven onward by some imp of the self-destructive perverse, some imp I hadn't encountered before in myself. ". . . . so oblivious," I said triumphantly, "to the patent fraud of some silver-tongued devil creeping up their metaphoric leg toward their . . ." I paused. I couldn't even guess at where I'd left daylight behind now. "*Why are women so* fey, so blithe, so egotistical as to believe . . ."

Ah, the loss of life. Not the Hindenburg but the black plague. I slumped into a chair having wrung out my life onto the floor and then stepped in it.

"Are you through?" she asked coolly.

Right here is where, in the past, I would have taken off with my best comedy routine about being possessed by evil spirits, about "how could I?", about prostration and unremitting repentance and lifelong indentured servitude I owed her for being such a reprobate one as I. I knew the words, she respected the riff, but nothing came out. My silence—the guillotine's swish. Off with my head.

* * *

Dr. S began haunting the gallery. He'd show up at first at the evening openings and made sure to greet me. "How's the article coming?" That was his standard, but he quickly turned to Marnie and alternately fawned, flattered and cooled it—the deadly trio. Then he began, she reported at first, dropping in during the day. Then Marnie stopped reporting that he'd show up during regular gallery hours. That was the beginning of the end, I think, because I helped out the ending.

Here's how I helped out. Jealousy, closely questioning her daily routine, and then pouting. It's the only way to describe what I did—teenage pouting. Nails in the coffin. But I couldn't stop. I knew every wrong move I was making, how it was driving her away, but I seemed incapable of stopping. Headlong, stumbling toward what I thought at the time was my own stupid, self-centered, immature reaction to Dr. S's interest in my Marnie. I think back now to his hand on my shoulder, my paralysis. That's when he planted this idiocy in me. It had to be. Somehow he rang all my bells, pushed all my buttons, and blew up my infrastructure all at the same time and reduced me, his competition for Marnie, to a thorough going nincompoop.

As she was packing up her things in boxes, I put all the pieces together, an act of inspired paranoia that, looking back, was really not that hard to figure out. That is, not hard to figure out if you will make the leaps of logic necessary for a bowl of gruel to inhabit an outlier scientist who then conceives of a lust for my girl and develops the superpowers to pull off the erotic coup. Now that I put it that way, I'm claiming insanity brought about by airborne spores and not enough exercise.

As I watched her tape up the final box, I asked where she was going to live. She informed me coldly that information of that sort would be henceforth (she didn't say "henceforth," of course) classified (she didn't say "classified"). She blew out the door saying she'd send for whatever she'd forgotten.

And there I was. Rex had won. Paradigm switch. The least (in terms of lines of complex code) had become the most. I went quickly through the "fuck this, fuck that" phase I had read about in books and seen on TV soaps. The existential crisis of loss of self was thorough, but mercifully brief.

From the fuck-it stage, I quickly began plotting my revenge. If I was going to believe that the Rex I knew first as a lump of goo had actually become the puppet master, then by God I was going to act within that realm of reality. A lump of goo had racial memory too—that was number one. Number two was that whatever had been done could be undone if I could get my shit together and do the doing. Number three, I'd assume that Marnie too had been replaced by Rex-tainted biochemical magic and not just grown tired of my kvetching. And finally, and this one was a supposition based on the whole weird logic of the affair, that Rex might grow tired of Marnie as he had those adventures in mutation that the paper kept reporting from around the world—mutant paint, roaring orchids, sentient dust, golden ponds. And that would be my advantage. I would never grow tired of getting back at that son of a bitch and his cavalier experiments on my species.

* * *

My article, of course, could contain none of this. My editor would call the men in white coats, and I'd be finished. I had to write up the article as if the world of science had a new star, Doctor Sewall, who with his new girlfriend on his arm, was taking the pre-Nobel bows at parties around the world. No, no, that was not going to get it done. I would solve the problem only by not acknowledging the problem. Never take on cosmic powers directly. That should be written over a doorway somewhere. Come at an angle. Sidle up. Insinuate and, like yon Cassius with his lean and hungry look, plot.

Racial memory: how much of the pre-striped incipience did

Rex remember? Did he remember the fundamental simplicity of his original code? I decided that he would be so fascinated by the keen and superior intelligence he'd come to be that he would not have the slightest interest in his origin myths, his days spent close to his aboriginal mud. He'd be drunk, I figured, with his seemingly endless possibilities. And I was right. It was a small article, again, but the logic was perfectly extendable out of Rex's etiology. The bastard couldn't help but just play around with his new realm. I was starting to use words like that, words I knew no editor would let me leave in. I realized that Rex-dust remained in me from the night that began it all. I'd have to watch out for more of that stuff.

Over the next week, I found three newspaper articles that I believed to be Rex at work. Or Rex playing around? Rex amusing himself? All of the above. Or at least in light of Marnie moving out, and I was pretty sure seeing Rex in the evenings, I attributed these three to Rex. One: A park ranger spotted then trapped what turned out to be a thirty-pound mallard duck. A four-pound mallard would be a big one. They ran mitochondrial DNA on it thinking it was the result of some crossbreeding with a Muscovy or larger duck. A large Muscovy male could weigh nearly twenty pounds. The extra ten pounds, though, had never been seen before. The science guys duly recorded it as a record, and, not incidentally, did not find Muscovy DNA in the giant mallard.

I thought, *Hi there, Rex. Out fooling around at the duck pond? Where did you get the time with all that conference running, that girl stealing?* The voices, yes. But this one was my own voice and merely pissed off.

Two and three: A dog was born in Mexico measuring two inches high, about half the previous record. Dogs have the greatest size variation of any mammal, and people since the domestication have been going for bigger and smaller. But always increments before this one. A little smaller, a little bigger. Then this Chihuahua the size of a cockroach. And that was number three on my list, the cockroach. The article declared it a "riding cockroach" measuring eight inches long. Again a quantum leap in size over the previous scale. Big duck, small dog, big cockroach—so what's the big deal? Nature (and by extension breeders) is always fooling around with the originals. A friend told me ur-pigs were great swimmers but that some hybrid modern versions have such short legs that they cut their own throats when they try to swim. English bulldogs have to have caesarean sections because they bred the birth canal out of the critter trying to make it look like Winston Churchill. Blah, blah, blah.

So? Coincidence you think? Big one, small one, big one—happens all the time. *The Guinness Book of World Records* lives off this stuff. I think it was the compression, these three in one week, me ready to see Rex in the biome, Rex the wooer, Rex the trickster. So I asked myself, why wouldn't he make a flock of thirty-pound mallards? I know I would. I'd cover the fucking sky with them and let the little humans quake below. I'd make the little dog vicious, the cockroaches legion and on the march across the Madagascar landscape eating villagers. I'd . . . sure I would. Me and all the horror filmmakers.

But Rex was perspicacious. Rex was just seeing what he could do. I'm sure everything Rex was responsible for was just for the sake of seeing it happen. He means us no harm. He just wants to be our benefactor. He loves us. He will send his only begotten . . . He will send His grace unto us and show us that we are His own.

Okay, I went that way for a while. I thought mythical, then biblical, then, finally, biological. I read a book many years ago by J. P. Donleavy called, *Meet My Maker the Mad Molecule.* Stories and sketches by the author, but the idea always appealed to me: all of human history is a cosmic joke—yes, the goof. And so, here we are free to gnaw our legs off trying to get out of various traps we've concocted for ourselves, or free to fondle ourselves to death in repeated orgasms because orgasm is all we really know of godhead. Or freedom, as Rex has shown us, to make thirty-pound mallards, two-inch dogs and riding cockroaches.

I cut out the three articles and set them on the coffee table separated by a sea of dark oak. I waited to see if they would squirm and then join up and then stick their collective tongue out. I brought a beer to the party. Then another and another while I waited for the scraps of articles to give me the word. Come on Rex, bring it on.

But like any god worth his mysteriousness, he did nothing more for a while than pick off my girlfriend. Marnie and Dr. S became an item. I guessed this by hiding out behind parked cars just across the street from the art gallery. I was hiding out long enough so that a Korean grocer came out and asked me if he could help me find what I seemed to be looking for under the cars parked in front of his grocery. I told him I was looking for my way. Inscrutable shit that he was, he tells me if I hadn't found my way the last three days, my way was certainly not here in front of his store. And that maybe I should look for my way in another place.

Dr. S was cutting quite the figure these days. He was sporting the skinny suit and tie, a little tweedy in the scarf area, some kind of Italian shoes that looked more like buttery slippers. Marnie too shone.

I became sure that Rex was behind and in front and around and in all this. Rex was a panoply of prepositions. I needed a plan.

How do you root out a genetic thief who actually hides out in the cells of your putative enemy? And what part of Rex had been inserted in what parts of my girlfriend and now was resident there too?

These rhetorical questions at first drove me to one of those adolescent plans I had always been prone to—the apocalyptic gesture. I would quit the whole fucking world and get gear. Then I would slide off into the closest wilderness area and wait while

Rex and whatever cohorts he could concoct took over humanity and humiliated them into being cosmic slaves. I wash my hands. I'm refusing to even participate in the battle. Bye!

But those great teen-age angst-ridden (back of hand to forehead here) gestures never last long in me, so I waited it out. Second wave was adult. I would pry that bowl of farina from his hiding places with all the resources available to me, and I would save myself and (not incidentally) humankind. I knew there was middle ground between the two, but my way, unlike the mature Buddha's, was never the middle way. I had to start with Marnie, I thought. Love was the way. I should have been listening to Tina Turner, however: what's love got to do with it?

Chapter VIII

I searched literature for a model: beauty and the beast? Anna Karenina? The bitch of Bucharest? Frau Blucher? Daisy Miller? Isolde? And so forth. I thought if I could find the ancient story, and then the new version of the primal utterance, then I could get Marnie back and begin the assault on Rex. I was still convinced that my possession theory was the only way to explain Dr. S's transformation. Fat government grants could not have done what I was seeing. I decided that the closest I could get to what happened was the idea of enchantment, that Marnie was an unwilling participant in the uncanny. Her will and, indeed, her very soul were not her own. As was my habit in times of chaos, I wrote down what my plans were to see how they looked on paper. That last phrase, "indeed, her very soul [was] not her own" stopped me cold. I could never have written that, at least without putting a quick line through it, before this Rex adventure. The prose wasn't mine. Was I part of the problem? Was I infested with Rex-ness too? I was trying to move the earth with no place to stand; I was the earth.

I decided that way lay madness. I had papers all over the kitchen table by this point and scrunched them all together and tossed them out. I was overcomplicating a really simple thing: if Rex were alive, he could also become dead. First order was to find Rex.

I tried calling Marnie. I claimed she had accidently taken a couple books I needed. No response. Then I began to stalk her, and finally "bumped into" her on the street. She kept looking at her phone to get the time, or to see an incoming text or something. But I asked her, for old time's sake if we couldn't have a quick coffee. I was trying out all my theories at once: possession, coercion, enchantment. She was clearly in a hurry to meet someone, him, or else just driven off by my ill manners—

what love falls to when it's no longer love.

Did she feel okay? She looked wan. Was she eating well? I was coming off like her mother, but I had to start someplace.

"To answer all your questions at once," she said slowly, "I'm fine, eating well, regular bowel movements, enough sleep. Thank you very much." She tapped on the face of her phone seeming to say: next question.

"Um, are you seeing a lot of Dr. Sewall?" I thought I'd jump in.

"Next question."

We used to play at interviewer/interviewee after I'd come home with tales of trying to get people to talk about their work, their lives, their opinions for articles. The classic one-word answers, like children give: yes, no, okay. Nope. I tried laughing it off.

"Okay, okay. Would you see me again if: (a) the end of the world was announced? (b) I did a cartwheel for you on the street? (c) I wrote a song then sang it publically for you while hopping on one foot?"

This business used to work, get her out of a funk, get me off whatever hook I'd hung myself on. She'd smile and it was done. Sometimes she'd make me sing some of the song I'd written for her. I'd make it up on the spot. She tapped her phone faster, staring right through me. Did I see Rex looking back at me? What wasn't funny about how I used to be funny?

"Look," she said. "I put up with a lot from you for a long time. It just wore out. Suddenly it just, I don't know . . . you know, *wore out*. It was like I was okay, just okay, and then I wasn't. I needed to go, get away. That's as clear as I can be." Tap. Tap. Tap.

What's love got to do with it? I was seeing in her face the reiterative quality of the fractal. It was a mask but a new mask. The same over and over again on all scales. I wound up the encounter with best wishes and happy holidays and stretched out a little toward her birthday. I huffed and puffed, and she was gone. And I was no closer. Dr. S had to be next. I'd assault the very fortress in which dwelt the King.

* * *

I skulked around, I'll admit—more than just the car business. In fact, I was skulking late one evening outside Marnie's apartment waiting for her to come home. And there wandering the street, probably waiting for her too I figured, was Dr. S. He was looking not so erect and studly, however. Some of the slump had returned. As he paced under the streetlight, he had a pallor to his skin I remembered from when he and his experiments resided in the Noah's Ark of the Ag building. He seemed confused. I thought, what the hell, let's see. What more do I have to lose?

The streetlight was making a perfect noir-novel cone of light and Dr. S passed in and out and then finally stopped directly in the middle of the cone, like a movie director would instruct him to do. I briefly hoped he might be beamed up into the streetlamp, and my tribulations would be finished. I came toward him from across the street.

"Good evening, Dr. Sewall," I said, as airily as I could. I was in the oh-hi-there mode, just walking down the street and by gosh there you were. I had hoped I had left all my skulk face on the other side of the street.

"Well, well, well . . ." he said. "I'm just . . . .you know . . ." Where the glib chat? Where the strut?

"She's not home yet. She always turns on all the lights in the place when she's there alone at night. Hell of an electric bill. But the tradeoffs were . . ." I stopped. Dr. S was looking down at his shoes as if he had lost a jewel down there.

Finally, he said slowly while looking up, "He lets me out sometimes. For a walk, he calls it. I go for a walk by myself. I always end up here. I thought he had some other business, but I don't know how it works. If he's not with me, where is he?"

The doctor looked at me, puzzled. As if I were supposed to

know immediately what the hell he was talking about. And then . . . of course, Rex. Rex let him out. So I said, "Rex." Not a question, just establishing the subject.

"Yes, directs the show, you know." He looked at me as if I should know about this show that is being directed.

"Tell me about the show."

"You know, the way he does things with me. Uses me to . . . what? To lift stuff. I'm his hands, so to speak. How could he lift anything without me? His fingers, don't you know. His radius. And his ulna." He laughed a sort of cackle, the kind he had when he sat in his old office chair with his feet up like a child.

"How long are you out for? Does he come and get you when he wants you back? Could you run away? How does he . . . ?" My interviewer skills all gone to pieces. All the questions at once—bad technique. Each question has an inside and you ask the outside one in order to get at the inside one. Then you ask your way into that one.

The doctor sighed. "I just know when I have to be back. That's all. I just know, and then I go back. I feel I have to. Have to be responsible to . . . what he wants. And then when we're together again, it's like we never were apart. Something like that. There's so much I don't know about the how. I *knew.* At first I knew everything. Rex was lines of code and . . . and . . . that other stuff, too. The agar-agar . . . and the booga-booga." The cackle again. "And the mojo . . ." He trailed off. "I believe you mentioned the mojo one time when you visited. Visited. That's what I do now. I visit. Then he visits. Then I get visited. Then . . ."

The light flickered like voices far away. And there we stood: I, waiting for something from him that wasn't really just a sigh; he, waiting to be called back by Rex. We waited. The world waited.

When I was eight years old, I first heard the phrase, "mind over matter." And being the literalist I was, I thought that if some people could do that, whatever it was, then I could. I went into the basement and let the helium out of a birthday-party balloon until it just hung in the air, going neither up nor down. Then I stared at it, elevated it, willed it up, hoped it up, threatened it up. There is, I thought, some *thing* you do to make your mind move matter. It must be like reading. At first you can't do it, then you can do it a little, and then you can do as well or better than anyone else. I remember it was something like a half hour later, my vision was getting blurred from staring. My wanting and yearning was wearing out from being yearned. And like those words on the page before I could read, nothing. Nothing! Eventually the balloon began to fall. I had succeeded in what . . . ? I thought. In pissing it off maybe. Did that count? Was that mind over matter?

Dr. S whirled suddenly and screwed up his face. "It's time. It's time. I have to get back. Nice seeing you. We'll have to do this again. Goodbye." And he walked off quickly lighting up at each cone of light until he was out of sight and diminished in the night.

What mind over matter was that, I asked myself? When I was eight, I remember feeling very foolish when I learned that humans could think their way to solutions to material problems—mind over matter. But I was also disappointed that the phrase meant something so drab and preachy. Oh that I could learn my way into some exclusive group that could move the world around with my mind. Apparently Rex had accomplished that trick, and Dr. S was now a mobile device that Rex rode around in like a meat taxi.

The article I was going to write was spattered across the night like a Whistler fireworks painting. I still had nothing to take to an editor, *less* than I had before. And Marnie came walking down the street.

She had apparently seen me as I stood and pondered what I had just experienced.

"Good evening. And good night, Jake. Are you stalking me?"

"I just ran into Sewall. Right here under this light. We had a talk."

"About?" She shifted her considerable purse to the other shoulder. It was a maneuver I had witnessed many times. We'd meet someone on the street, someone I knew and she didn't, and she'd begin the encounter with the shift: the big bag swung across her body like she was clearing space, ready for the dance of introductions. This swing had the snap of frying the air between us and establishing the new distance of ex-lovers.

I asked, "Do you two, you and Sewall, ever talk about Rex? You remember Rex, don't you?" Try out that gambit.

She clutched the purse to her body like armor. And then finally said, "Yes, I do. I remember Rex. You told me a lot about Rex."

"But did Sewall tell you about Rex? Did he tell you about how Rex . . ." Where would I go with this? How weird was I allowed to get? I was on very thin ice with her in any case. Should I just put on a clown nose, skip off throwing daisies, have her call the white coats? "Well, about Rex the experiment? Or Rex the entity . . . ?" Not that way. Not that way. "Or Rex the DNA code, the RNA instructions?"

She said, "He told me about Rex in a sort of abstract way. Why? Is there something wrong with . . . with the Rex principle? I guess, that was my impression of Rex—a principle that was the basis for much of his work. Look, I have an early day tomorrow. Did you want to say something to me? Don't ask me to come back. Or does that jump ahead too fast?"

"No. I get it. Crazy acting makes everyone uncomfortable. Doesn't get anything solved. I just wanted to say that, well, that Sewall is having trouble with Rex—the principle, the idea, maybe. So keep that in mind when you two—"

"Us two? You think we're a couple now? Nice one. I should jump from one whacky to another whacky? I'll tell you what." The purse swung by on its way to the other shoulder. "I'm doing just fine, thank you very much. Just fine. I'm enjoying the loneliness. Yes. The loneliness. I get lonely and then sort of fit myself around it. It's nice in the same way the energy in a good painting is nice—disturbing but full of energy. Like that. So if you don't have anything else to say, I'd like to get to bed."

I stayed under the streetlight until all the lights in her apartment were ablaze and staving off the night spirits and swampy miasmas. I followed Dr. S's route down the street toward home.

About halfway back home, I saw Dr. S ahead standing, swaying slightly between streetlights. I stopped and watched. He was caught between two lights and cast a shadow in both directions, like he was propped up on the two oval shadows. I watched him for a full minute then walked slowly toward him. He didn't see me coming because as I got closer I could see his eyes were closed. He seemed to dance to unheard music, his face a kind of beatific smirk like the oldest of Buddhas. I stood very close to him to see if he would sense me. But no, he continued the dance. I cleared my throat, and slowly, slowly he opened his eyes as if awakening.

"Oh, hi Jake," he said like a stoner coming to. "Nice night."

I stepped back and watched him come all the way out. He stopped swaying and stood with his hands on his hips.

"Yeah, nice night," I said too. We had established that it was a nice night. "Where were you just now?"

"I was . . . let's see. I was . . . hum. Maybe not where. Maybe what. No, how. How is where I was." He laughed, swayed a little as if to remember better. "I was . . . occupied. I was being occupied! I was moving back in."

The slump was gone. The charm back. The glow, the mojo—all that stuff. Rex was back, I assumed. But it was like the doctor was drunk, his system overloaded by some drug, and he was holding on to his equilibrium just by threads. So I thought I'd go directly for the interview.

"Rex, if I might be so bold? How do you do that? Occupy?

How'd you move back in? I was talking to Dr. Sewall very recently, and he told me he had been let out for a while by himself."

There was a considerable pause, and he looked at me without blinking, maybe screwing with me for the zombie effect. His hair that had been flying off Einstein-style twenty minutes earlier was now well behaved and civil. And the biggest difference besides the slump-absence was the skin glow. Occupied, indeed. There was somebody else in there, somebody with much better skin than Doctor Sewall.

"Oh, Jake," he began, apostrophe forward. "Jake, Jake, Jake. You act as if Rex and Sewall are two different things. They're not. Try to think additively. Is nine different from five plus four? They're both nine. Nine this. Nine that. See? Let's try again. Seven plus two?"

My first reaction to his condescension was to call him a condescending prick. Of course. But there was nothing after that. Where would I go then?

He took me by the arm and started to walk me toward the next streetlight. "How Rex always worked—since the beginning—was by adding himself to something else. Your head voices. A slime mold. An orchid in the jungle. A duck." He kept looking at me to see if I was following.

"And . . . ?" This was an old interviewing trick implying there was more to be said on the subject, a sub-subtext waiting to be unearthed.

"Soooo. So, I think you can see that Rex needs something to be added to. Otherwise, well, he's a rudimentary set of instructions. He needs the multiplier! The complexity of a host. Have you ever wanted, say, for five minutes to be a lion?" Then the actor came out; he crouched. "Bringing down that wildebeest, that first crunch through the neck, the thing still quivering, the warm blood taste going all the way into your spine with delight? Or if that doesn't appeal to you, how about just a hummingbird swooping up into a vertical climb doing the mating flight, hanging there for a second, then slamming toward the earth to swoop and do it again. Now take the slime mold." He was still airborne, a hummingbird then swooped into slime mold.

We walked along. He assumed a rich, paternal, teacher voice, and I the acolyte alongside. "Ah, the slime mold," I said. "Got to be less interesting."

"But no. No. Not less interesting at all. Come with me. Nope, I shouldn't take you." He looked me in the eye. "Yet." And he laughed. "But imagine with me the slime mold casting back and forth between animal and plant. Right at the second when the entire organic substance goes one way or the other to survive. Wow. But even more wow is if you could be there and go back and forth, back and forth—just fooling around, mind you—just to feel it over and over. Plant. Animal. Plant. Animal. Look out realms and empires! The slime mold itself can't . . . doesn't have to do that flashing back and forth. But, what if you could? Wouldn't you do it like self-indulgence of the highest order? Whee! I'm a plant. I'm an animal. Cosmic masturbation, I tell you. It feels so fine."

And, yes, he did begin to sing the last part. I kept thinking, shit, where's my tape recorder now? "So could you go into anything? I mean, Rex?"

"Oh, maybe maybe maybe. But why? Pick and choose. Pick and choose. Let's talk trees. The xylem and the phloem—pretty much fun. Stuff going places, chugging along. But the heart wood, that takes patience and a kind of appreciation for the long run. It's learnable, and frankly, worth the learning to appreciate. But if you've done it once, you've done it. Know what I mean? The long, flat sine wave. The waiting? The long view of petty things in general."

He stopped and took me by the shoulders as if he were prepping me for a kiss goodnight.

"So Jake, wouldn't you? Of course you would. And then after

a while you'd go back and do the greatest hits again. Lion, for sure. Shark and seal—not as much fun as it looks since sharks are . . . well, so basic, if you know what I mean. Basic is okay, though. You get to look after a while for synapses to occupy. You get to crave the action, you see. The slam bang, the merry-go-round of it. You usually get some of that with mammals. Some of your stinging critters, the nematocysts, the fiery ants, then way out there with the asps and mambas and pit vipers and . . ."

He trailed off, almost dreamy, maybe recalling a fine day's kill. But then . . .

"Jake, are you buying this? Has the narrative got some appeal? I mean the story: Rex conquers the universe from the platform of a string of computer code? Kind of good, isn't it? So . . . ? You in?"

I was back on my heels suddenly. Is he shitting me? Has he been shitting me all along? Do I get the big laugh now? What I got was a slap on the back, sort of a laugh. And then the gotta-go looking at his watch.

"More later, Jake. Jake? More later, I promise."

I had been intrigued, courted, seduced, fucked and kissed goodnight. Had I? All so quickly I couldn't entirely recall all that happened. The interview, fake or not, had its very high moments. Did I buy it? The big IT, the premise? Oh, yeah. Yes I did, and not only buy it, I found myself looking forward to the next date.

* * *

Now that I was used to the looking, I never had to look far to see Rex abroad in the world. Of course, my own growing paranoia helped fill in the pieces. I conceded the night to Doctor Sewall. I conceded the night to any other forces and demons and *duendes* and mysterious shit that wanted to claim any part of the victory. Sometimes the weird shit wins hands down. My voices fell silent and, worse, morosely silent as if they all turned their vocal backs and sulked. And skulked away. Guys? Where the hell are your irrational lovelinesses? Where the jokester who calls me by my name? Where the brightening air into which all wonder blows like the dust from butterfly wings?

I'd say I walked home, but I didn't. I wandered and on the way hooked up the narrative-maker. I needed a story that would contain all this mess, that would hold like a bowl all the weird fruit tumbling into my life. A story could.

I walked and wrote.

Most of them seem to be able to use only one hand with any skill. The right side. Some few of them, about 10 or 11 percent based on observed samples use the left. And very few can use both hands with skill as we do. Sometimes we see them holding some object in the dominant hand and then when needing to do some skill they will transfer the object to the weak hand in order to use the skilled hand. We think this weakness can be used to our advantage when the time comes.

I walked with one foot off the curb so that I bobbed, high-low, high-low like a limping drunk.

They have an idea that a separate "self" is somehow constructed or inherent (not clear yet which) and that each individual has a lifelong goal to first find out what the self is and then to cultivate it. They spend an immense amount of time in the wealthier nations doing this cultivation and informing their young that this is the value of being alive—the pursuit of this fabricated "self." Here is a representative case. I sat at a nearby table recording this. I have used the names they usually call their dogs because . . . well, because I think it fitting.

Their young. Their young. I'll certainly keep that.

Rob and Maggie are sitting at a table outside a café in the afternoon. Rob speaks of what bothers him at his workplace. He says that his bosses want his "self" instead of just his labor. They want to crush the self into some larger enterprise in the name of profit. They want to use him up and then spit him out some figurative door without his self, but with some compensation for his participation in their goals. He complains to Maggie bitterly. He seems to think there is some form of death, some pre-death in this process. Some horror that will precede his actual death. The illusion of the self seems to be thorough and conclusive. Rob is an adult approximately thirty years old and repeatedly mourns himself to Maggie. She listens and nods. She has dressed in such a way as to distinguish herself from other females. She is, I think, doing the same thing as Rob is doing with words. She is continuing the narrative of the self in colors and cloth arrangements. Her shoes she keeps removing and then dandling on her toes because apparently they are uncomfortable but distinguishing of the perceived self. Rob has used words like "soulless" and "wrung out" and (repeatedly) "scream" ("I could just scream, I want to scream, I hear myself screaming silently in the meeting . . ."). My recommendation is that when the time comes we use this self-induced anguish. It seems painful, and we should be able to offer them either the chance to get away from the anguish of self (I personally don't think this will work since the self concept is so heavily ingrained) or, better, offer them the chance to pursue a genuine self or an authentic self, what one of their writers called "an original relationship with the universe." The other observers and I have repeated this phrase to each other many times and it never fails to amuse us. Once when we had gathered to discuss them, I began the meeting with: "We have come together today"—and then I paused and watched the observers' faces—"to establish an original relationship with the universe." Great hilarity broke out and it was nearly five minutes before order could be restored and we could proceed with our observations.

We should be able to offer every adult and the more advanced young ones these fictive goals. Our plans should always include what version we are able to concoct of this elusive self. It will take more study to find exactly what buttons we have to push to offer them a genuine self, but we all think it will be worth the effort eventually. The amazing thing is that across the many cultures we have studied here, this self-business seems universal. No matter what sacrifices are asked in repressing the self under various conditions like war, this "self" fiction persists. It's as if they simply won't continence the alternative. The truth: they are all the same. One of our members put forward the idea that we might confront them with this truth and that would be more effective, when the time comes, in disarming them entirely. The rest of us thought it would just make them angry and recalcitrant so deeply believed is the cultural fraud. We might try his theory on some captives to see what happens.

The other side to the fabrication of the self is the way they have all embraced some idea of the elusive and non-apparent soul. Originally concocted by a number of Greek philosophers approximately in the 5th century BCE, the soul has persisted as a way of distinguishing them from the rest of the living world. Some of what they call the "primitive religions" have not allowed a separate soul for humans and for the other living and nonliving things of the earth. The result is that these primitive religions have kept a continuance between people and the nature around them. And so what happens to one happens to all. This version of soul seems to us superior if equally mistaken at the base. The consequences of this continuous soul linking all things provides better results than the separate soul fiction. Either way though, the soul enterprise can be used when the time comes.

As a consequence of the previous observations, they educate their young as if each were a complete blank slate upon which the collected history of their kind must be slowly and painfully written by education. Each young human must spend countless uncomfortable hours ingesting the fictions, the narratives of its people. Again, there is no continuity since each one must be filled individually, and though some are more apt and more easily filled than others, the net result is much waste and no conservation of energy. When the time comes, I hope many of them will see our way as infinitely superior and efficient. They really won't have a choice, but it would be more pleasant all around if, when the time comes, they just saw the truth suddenly and consented.

I could feel the high commander, or whatever he was, percolating in the story. I waited for a piece of late-night traffic to pass and felt I could lift the cars with my mind and get them out of the way. If I wanted to. If they interfered again. If it pleased me.

Next, the entire sexual business. Though there seems to be some range in size though virtually none in position, our locker room cameras have confirmed that there are only the two kinds of them. Through the information from our other cameras, we can also confirm that no matter what combination of male and female—two of the same kind, one of each kind, any number of each or a combination—there is apparently a limited range of activities given the original equipment. Our researchers were interested to learn the wide range of outside equipment they bring into the act, but essentially there are still possible only the activities initially associated with the anatomical equipment. And here comes the strange part: given these limitations—our sexual condition has far fewer restrictions since our parts are much more adaptable—they create the same kind of fictions they have about the self and the soul, but this time about sex. They have multiple names for all the potential combinations of participants doing *the same things to each other.* They seem to insist on right and wrong combinations of the truly limited equipment as if they somehow require an incorrect story and a correct story about very tiny differences. This baffled many of our observers—the strife, the pain, the shunning, the guilt and blame associated with proscribed combinations of activities. When the time comes there will, I should imagine, be general rejoicing among all people when we give them the gift of sexuality, their own sexuality, of course, since we are not fit to reequip them all entirely. Oh that we were! But that is not in keeping with our directive.

When the time comes, we expect great rejoicing on all sides, but for now we continue to observe. For example, we found the water of earth to be of truly uneven quality. If you accumulate more wealth, you drink better water. The graphs are conclusive—x-axis increasing wealth, y-axis increasingly more pure water—rising perfect graph line. And with human metabolism there was then a perfect correlation between cellular health and wealth, epigenetics, then healthier offspring. While historical exceptions did occur, viz. the Romans and lead poisoning, the key observation of our fieldworkers was that we can use the water observations nicely when the time comes. There is, clearly, no better battlefield than water. It is convenient for us that we will have such a focused center for our activities when the time comes. In past situations in other places, other worlds, we have had sometimes so many different fronts that our ultimate energies were diluted across multiple key conquests, and certain difficulties (and casualties) were incurred. With the earth's water, we have a natural focus for our efforts when the time comes. They are, it seems, perfectly thirsty for our purposes.

Our fieldworkers. Maybe that was my role. The fieldwork. I'd report back, sometimes just make shit up, tell the committee whatever I wanted, just to see what would happen.

Coffee, and in some parts of the world, tea, present interesting possibilities. These are ritual stimulants, apparently, and large segments of the populations seem habituated if not addicted. By ingesting one or two cups of liquid people report that they are "okay," or "that's more like it," as if some sort of completion has taken place. The important fact here seems to be that they were not okay before ingesting or that something essential was lacking that was completed by the coffee. In committee, we pondered adding a few DNA strands to the world's coffee beans, apparently fairly easy to do according to our science people, in order to introduce a few alternative reactions to what we've come to call the "okay syndrome." When the time comes the excitability engendered by the coffee can be directed to our purposes so that wherever there is morning in the world, our directives will be met with complicit and excited humans. The retailer, Starbucks, is a perfect place to begin since it seems to be an ubiquitous delivery system for what is being called the "new coffee." That part of the world where tea is favored will be even easier to redirect since there seems to be only one tea variety responsible for most of the tea. There seems also to be a number of non-tea or coffee drinkers. I believe these will be of no real consequence when the time comes.

The Starbucks was closing; a few customers had to be rousted apparently, in order to close up.

One of our operatives has suggested that the car, specifically out of all the possible vehicles public and private, has reached cult status among humans, that those without cars yearned to have one, that those with inexpensive cars yearned to have more expensive ones, and that those able to drive very expensive cars wanted to have more of them. This observation, if borne out by research, will be useful when the time comes since any pattern of yearning has proven valuable in the past. Many languages of the earth have special forms and modes to express this yearning since the yearning itself has come to be identified with being human. The subjunctive or optative mood is what we find everywhere there is language. Part of the self discussed above is contingent on the recognition of humans as creatures that long after what they don't have or know. This longing, of course, accounts for their knowledge base as well as the self-deception that marks their activity involved in seeking some kind of "authentic" self—their science and their religion, their illusions and their realities. When the time comes, this *yearning after* can be a key component in our enterprise. It seems that this wanting/yearning/wishing/hypothetical mood of humans is thoroughly part of each living specimen so that we have found no example high or low in intelligence, high or low in financial condition, that is without a substantial and essential portion of this business. When we know a trait, and especially a trait so perfectly distributed as this one, we can use it when the time comes. Configurations have been very useful to us in the past.

Our report would be incomplete without dealing with the tricky bits or inconsistencies of humans, those characteristics that might present problems when the time comes. I begin with what they have lumped together and called love. It is at once the most thoroughly imbued trait and the most fraudulent. It contains a little bit of everything I've mentioned—self, soul, purity of water, overstimulation of coffee, and sex. All these fictions come together and join up as the greatest fiction of them all: love.

Ah, love. What was it again? Maybe the way light fell through the cracks in the universe that sometimes made funny glows and then that was love.

As we found out in the past, whether some beliefs were based on reality or complete cultural concoction, it is not relevant when the time comes. This love business presents itself as an immense barrier to easy transition. From the smallest version—I love ice cream—to the most thoroughly encompassing love of a person for family or God or even self, love will have to be factored into the final formula for this world. We need to accommodate it, maybe even say yes to it publically at first, and then probably we'll have to deal with its extinction by fully replacing it with a more substantial alternative. I think that our previous methods might not work here. The old switcheroo, as they like to say: we give them something that on the surface looks like what they're fond of, and then slowly, slowly take that one away while slipping our alternative into its place. "This carob is just as good as chocolate," our sociologist likes to say with a laugh.

The habit of self-stimulation among them seems to cross cultures and languages. Apart from sex, they all look for something new even if the result of the new experience is worse than what it replaces, worse than nothing at all. We discovered a line in one of their songs, "I'd rather feel bad than feel nothing at all." We will in time, of course, invite them to feel just that—nothing at all, a kind of cosmic heroin, I suppose. And so, when the time comes, there will have to be a significant redirection of what they are fond of calling human nature. What they mean by that is not entirely clear, but since we know we have to subvert what they think it is eventually, here are some speculative notions on what they might mean by human nature: (1) By an act of faith previous to any logic, many of them believe that human nature is separate from Nature-nature and by this separation they create for themselves a category in the natural world that is not open to any other flora or fauna. Apparently keeping all other living things out of this category is the central imperative and defining parameters for this category. It is a *sui generis* category that insists that including anything except humans would nullify the category completely. See the fictions about the soul above. (2) Human nature is precarious and though it is generously allotted to all humans, during times of war, one defined group can take it back from another group to more easily slaughter that group without moral repercussions. Their Bible documents a number of cases of this phenomenon. Their recent history is full of instances whereby one group (e.g., Catholics or Protestants, or Muslim and Christian, or two kinds of Catholics—an ancient or orthodox one and a newer or Roman one) withdraws the privileges of being human and returns the enemy to nature, effectively kicking that group out of the privileged category and into one with "lower" animals. It seems mass killing is made easier under the conditions of this redefinition. When the time comes, this will be a valuable distinction we can harness. They will certainly understand the distinction immediately. (3) Human nature can include but is not limited to essentialisms. That is, because of the flexible nature of definitions of this particular form of nature, people themselves have created what they call political entities to create official or state-supported versions. That is, if any definition gets particularly complex and difficult to manage because of too many exceptions, too many if-thens, the state steps in and simplifies the definition by the act of ridding the definition of its complexity, subtlety and nuance and replacing these with gross features that then constitute the official definition. This official act is a corollary to the condition of war that allows one group to remove the other group's human status and return them to the realm of animals and plants. (4) Human nature, it turns out, is a thinly veiled kind of arrogance that the species cultivates. And a key to understanding human nature as they use it may well be for us to examine the arrogance itself.

I was just going to let all that stuff out, too. Why the fuck not? I was all the way into the gutter now until I saw a police patrol car ahead and thought I'd better do the sidewalk for a while. I was sleepy for a bit but was now wide awake and in full concocting mode.

Inside the arrogance first is fear. The same fear is apparent when they view a place of particular beauty, or majesty. Their first impulse is to lose the fragile self they've constructed because it is puny in the scale of majestic and beautiful nature. So immediately they declare the place holy and reduce it to creeds and dogmas that come with organized holiness. That act contains the majesty, restores the self to grander size (after all the religion is a product of those same selves) and drives away that fear of dissolution. Name the place (e.g., Delphi in Greece) and reduce it to the priesthood's cartography. Then there they are, slapping of hands, and they all feel undiminished. When the time comes, I recommend we use majesty, the scale of it, to our ends.

I believe it is important, as it has been in the past, for us to understand any people's origin stories. The study of these stories has yielded, in more than one case, a piece of the cultural puzzle that proved crucial when the time came. For example, one group not on earth, saw themselves as having been exonerated completely by supernatural powers of their own invention so that the entire group was enfranchised as sort of lower-level gods—blameless for all previous error, favored by all the powers they could then subsequently invent, and, above all, superior to even their own natural extinction in death. When the time came, they proved a very resilient people, like rainwater or dust or some other naturally occurring element. Elemental, yes. That's what made them difficult.

But humans have universally conceived of themselves as faulty because they die. They see themselves as punished and unworthy of even the continuity of rainwater, wind, seasonally falling leaves. They see themselves as beholding to the whim or grace or unfathomable kindness of great powers other than themselves. So they sacrifice and trade ritual acts for God's forgiveness—forgiving them for what they merely are. This fact is an extraordinary leverage for us. We don't even need to deceive them into thinking we ARE those whimsical powers. Since they conceive of these in such a variety of ways, we might have some trouble acting out all the variations on the themes. But we don't have to. Their enormous sense of inferiority is sufficient to our ends. Weak, small, puny insufficient humans: only temporary experiments with grandeur—it was labeled historically as arrogance—pop up here and there. Most appear under the rubric of what they called Romanticism. All were eventually condemned. We should have no trouble when the time comes harnessing the word "mere" in mere humans.

That might be just crabby, but it stays in if I can make it stay in.

One origin story is instructive, and we should keep it in mind. The Mayan group created a story that began four steps earlier than any other creation story. Most origin stories begin with emptiness then move into filling the creation. But the Mayans, in their story-performance called the Popol Vuh, begin four steps before the void. The gods, two of them, try out creation three times before hitting on a suitable version of humans—the people made of corn. Trial creation number one, after having created the animals, was the mud people who immediately tried an assault on the two creators and so the creators sent a flood to wash away and dissolve the dangerous mud people. Next try was the stick men who proved so boring—they had no souls, no minds they said—that the gods grew bored with them and sent them back into nature along with the reed women created for them. The people made of corn proved satisfactory: for constant worship, to feed the immense egos of the two gods, to provide more of themselves. Just right.

While the Christian, Buddhist, Mayan, Muslim, Hindu and especially the Kalapuya Indian versions each have their charm—a void, then an active agent (God, Turtle, Thunderbird, etc.)—they all leap immediately to making sacred worship a feature of each life. I think we will find it useful to study this pattern well before the time comes since universal patterns in the past have always been the keys to our successful enterprises. The Mayan version postulates an error-prone, egomaniacal, childlike eternal power, as often do the other creation stories when they don't substitute an angry father who creates on a whim. The logic here is the key. When the time comes, we will choose a way to appear to them. We will choose a collective personality, and the most efficient one we can choose is one that is immediately recognizable to the largest segment of the human population. Child or angry father—or a combination—will do. But whatever we choose, I recommend an immense and immeasurable ego and sense of privilege that the most successful gods have. Humans need to serve, to worship, to sublimate themselves into a larger plan. We can do this for them when the time comes.

I have been working recently on a more abstract project. The present version of Western culture—Europe and what they call "The New World" especially—seems to have collectively grasped on to what I have come to call *outrageousness*. We see everywhere attempts by individuals to decorate themselves in ways that will draw to them the attention of others. I don't mean what they call style or fashion (we have a full report on that in another document elsewhere). Here is the abstraction. Our observations include various forms of self-mutilation in which ink is injected somewhat painfully under their skin and a variety of metal devices pierced through the skin as tokens of something. It's not clear. But our present portmanteau word is "outrageousness." It seems a significant part of the population will . . . no, that's not the right word. The concept is better conveyed in "need." They need to be considered outrageous by the others around them. There seems a special satisfaction, a gratification and yearning fulfilled in this outrageousness. Our studies show that maybe there is even a fundamental saving of the particular self in becoming this perceived outrageous: a gratification very close to the needs for food and water and maybe even sex. Comparable anyway. Our scientists are having trouble understanding the potency of this outrageousness. Tattoos and piercings are only two of the ways outrageousness is cultivated. Very big, very loud—any of a number of excessives—accompany very expensive, very rare, very illegal and very ugly/beautiful. The humans seem to receive from outrageousness some of what we have termed "mother's milk" in studying other worlds. While their societies run on a perceived center, an even keel, a moderation of both cause and effect, the surreptitious individual agenda is excess and outrageousness. The group form of this is war. Though they consider war idiosyncratic, it is in fact the long-established norm. War is the way societies come to define themselves—outrageous behavior as "normal." When the time comes there will have to be preparations, as we have made other times and other places, for the bellicose norms of humans. And as we have done in the past, we can use their inclination toward conflict to lead them to the precise point of the arrival of the "moment" in time, time arrived. It hasn't failed yet, our jujitsu use of their momentum against them. It's always delightful to watch for the exact moment when they realize what has happened, how their own force has succeeded against them.

One step at a time, I thought as I was going home, but I'm wandering. And wondering.

Our group is nearly through with its various studies. There are, however, a few puzzles that remain. Some percentage of them seem capable of a peculiar ability to embrace no belief whatsoever. Or rather they embrace the lack of belief or emptiness itself as if it could stand in the place of religions, love, the soul, even optimism as an abstract. This ability we have not encountered in other instances, other worlds. It seems an aberration in this one. It could be the same percentage as left-handedness, and that might be the pattern that reveals a constant variation in their world, the 10 percent rule maybe, though I have thought to name it after myself since I noted the correspondence to frequency of left-handedness. And we find it compellingly powerful in a number of ways. This ability to hold dear the absence of any evidence of God's presence—it is an absence that we feel has a presence. Power comes from the suspension, the waiting, the balancing on a knife's edge without plunging off in either direction into some prepackaged belief or another. The temptation must be just as powerful to relent, to go along with the comforting and prepared narratives of creeds and doctrines and dogmas. We find this 10 percent both interesting and, frankly, harrowing, because when the time comes, this group will become, *could* become a significant problem. Our ancient wisdom has always radiated from one single revelation now lost in time itself—that there is no actual. The corollaries that logically flow from this key to reality account for everything we are, everything we've become—past present future. The 10 percent have the capability to . . . well, interrupt us when the time comes. Derail. And so, the question arises about how to identify this small segment of humans, how to reduce their numbers so whatever perceptions they are capable of when the time comes will not interfere in any meaningful way. They are small in percentage but a significantly large number when calculated globally. What to do with them? How to, perhaps, discredit them in front of the others. Another Inquisition but this time on a bigger scale. We have to find a way to identify these people. Alas, left-handedness is not useful in any way. Only the percentages of the population seem about the same. If we could detect the propensity by our standard readouts, if it ran in families, if it were located on the DNA, if factors in its presence were environmental. . . . But so far we have no etiology. It has random distribution, irrational association, no formal pattern.

And so with everything else ready, we still have this wild card in favor of the humans. And when the time comes we will see just how the scenario plays out. That's my view. My superiors are in favor of taking no chances and continuing study on the 10 percent we think might be fatally dangerous to our project. I defer to them, of course, because they have been right to be thorough in the past. But I can't help but harbor a curiosity, a powerful curiosity I admit, about what would happen if we just went ahead when the time comes. What would be the result of the 10 percent resistance? Would they be enough to sabotage the entire enterprise? I think I am only this curious because we have succeeded so well in the past. I self-accuse and see that my curiosity is idle and maybe even playful and does not fit in a serious situation. Still . . . I wonder.

We'll see. The time has come.

And I damn sure want to be there for it, too. They wouldn't dare do it, of course, without me. I wouldn't let them. But, alas, maybe the time has come. Rex? You listening?

Chapter IX

The next manifestation of Rex was not so playful. It turns out his curiosity was not only boundless, but absolutely amoral. *The New York Times* rarely has short articles, but this one was. In the "Science Tuesday" section appeared a report on a scientific breakthrough that seemed to get away from the researcher. In an attempt to contrive bacteria that would eat metal and return it to a pure state, the researchers at Abbott-Limberg Labs in Germany had accidentally produced a second generation of the bacteria, an offshoot or error in the production of the original that had escaped through the plastic restraining walls and begun to eat internal combustion engines. Something about the contiguous oil and metal made the actual engine much more desirable for the bacterium than just the metal. The oil acted like mayonnaise, I guess. This second generation also ate plastics, as it did to escape, while the original was completely contained by plastics. For forty days and forty nights, biblically enough, the well oiled engines of European highways beginning with Germany, were brought to a standstill. The engines were pitted like Swiss cheese, completely eaten through where the oil was most available. All electric cars were spared. Electric trams and trains were spared. And then the eating stopped. The bacteria had run its course. It was over. It was Rex, of course, but could I hail the world and tell my story? You see, I would begin. I went to interview a guy who had a bowl of gray oatmeal and . . . No, there were enough competing versions of what happened. And Europe was perfectly willing to blame the Germans for everything and other ills besides. After all, it was a German scientist in South America who did the breeding on Africanized bees, wasn't it? Here they go again, was the general consensus. Why should we be surprised?

My take on the whole forty-day catastrophe was that Rex had moved from harmless fooling around into the realm of paradigm-changing experiments. He had, I figured, the earth by the short hairs. Yes, those short hairs. And was giving a yank to see what would happen, how we'd react.

We, I mean all of us, reacted by concocting competing stories, letting our narratives vie with each other. The weak minded used the oldest stories since they were available: God's vengeance for our failure to . . . (fill in your own favorite sin or moral failing here), or the long predicted apocalypse is finally here and Hallelujah. Next came the second-generation stories that accounted for the particulars of the "accident": the Frankenstein punishments for messing around with the natural—the GMO-into-monster eventuality—then the aliens and new masters who have made their presence known to us finally. And then there were the most contrived explanations of paradigm shifts in nature that were inevitable: global warming, overpopulation, inattention to great and striving variety of Darwinian life-principle. I figured that last one was the closest to getting at Rex. And "Rex!" was what I wanted to shout from the metaphoric rooftops.

Here's the shit that was flowing my way. My editor had essentially fired me, told me to go to hell with my delays and "just-a-minutes." Marnie had left town on a vacation that I figured might never end. The art gallery told me she had taken a "sabbatical." Dr. S was unavailable and in conference and would get back to me and would like any questions submitted by email and . . . just like that I was floating.

The only thing I could think to do was return to Dr. S's former office in the Ag building. Maybe he had left something there I could use to make sense of what I couldn't make sense of. I couldn't get anywhere near his new office; the guardians he had posted sealed off all the outer and inner layers of access. I alone knew it was Rex and not the poor old schlub I first met with his bowl of trick goo. Either that or my own delusions had finally ganged up on me, cut my mooring ropes, and set me adrift.

In the Ag building, I felt the urge to hail the stock by name, pat the sleeping grad student on the hay bales, hoot and moo and squeak and honk my way through, because I wasn't sure what I was doing there if it wasn't the equivalence of mooing at the fluorescent lights.

Dr. Sewall's old office had the writing scraped off the window, the plate removed from the door. I pushed it open. Took a deep breath and went in. It smelled like socks. Pretty clean socks but socks all the same. This little piggy went to market all right.

His desk was still there in the same place. The file cabinets had been emptied—I checked immediately. And way back in the corner where Rex's Lucite cage had been, there was something. The light was flickering in the bad-fluorescent mode, with the blue-orange shift and some hum and crackle. Rex's corner was empty, or so I thought at first. I wished I had brought a flashlight. I thought I heard a voice say "over here" but I hear my name and the voices all the time. And again, they don't tell me to do bad things or threaten me. Taken as an average, the two words, "over here," are some of the most common of all the voices. I think of them as merely pointing out the world, as if the world had supplied a voice-over for me, a guide. So I heard "over here" like an old friend saying, "You won't believe what I saw today." I've been alive long enough to know that not everyone has a voice—*any* voice—going on in his head. But I also know, as I've said, those Augustinian voices in people's heads prove God's existence—our God who we are not to presume to understand (cf. the book of Job).

"Over here" again and there was Rex. Or sort of Rex. In the corner where he had formerly been a gray blob awaiting his stripes was a teaspoon of what looked like dried rye bread. It was sufficient, it appeared, to send out a signal.

"Rex? I asked. "Is that you?"

And here I would like to be as careful as I can in relaying what went on. I often answer the voices—and so do you. Some of you.

And in many ways this was no different. I was talking to rye breadcrumbs in a most affable way. "How are? How're you doing?" But also, given the disappearance of Dr. S, the German engine fiasco, the dust of this, the flowering of that, the seeping together of all the thin layers of the world, I was ready for the extraordinary dressed up as the mundane. Rex said: "I just came back for a while . . . to my roots, you see. Here's where it started. For me, anyway. It's one of the places it always starts. And stops. It starts and stops and starts. Always starts again. But I think of Dr. Sewall as a kind of father, a progenitor. My ancestor. But the more I ponder it, I have had so many fathers, so many . . ."

And then the discourse broke off the same way it does when I'm writing. It faded and it was up to me to make it go again, reconstitute it out of what came before. So I asked Rex back.

The light flicker was now, it seemed, about ten times what it had been. As when you begin to hear a fan or a steady squeak somewhere, then you can't stop hearing it. And it gets louder and more insistent. I began again hearing Rex, his apologia.

"You want reasons? I'll give you reasons as soon as you show me where reason lies. I'll dig it out if you'll point it out. Don't even start with me. I just came back to see what I can see. I'm using the light fixture as a power source. Really just screwing around. I could just as well use you as use the light bulb—what's the difference really? But florescent light is kind of a carnival ride for things like me. The swooping and humming and buzzing—great fun. The time had come, you see."

I should have gone into interview mode, but I didn't. I should have questioned him closely about the metal/oil business, would it be back? I should have at least run him into a few corners and made him put up or shut up. What were his plans for world domination? Was there a weakness we could exploit? (Okay, I should have saved that one for a subtext of the questioning.) What were his politics? Good one. Everyone would want to know that—whose side he was on. Did he plan to reproduce? Another good one—sex sells even if it's asexual reproduction or something even slicker.

Time went by, and I was staring into the corner. The light had become steady in that garish way of tube lights. I blinked and blinked to get a better view. I found myself alone. I wanted to ask him if I could see him again somehow, call him up for a proper interview, be my Commissioner Gordon to his Batman, Jimmy Olsen to his Superman. All I could hear eventually was mooing with the occasional poultry exclamation. I felt sleepy, like I'd just worked out and needed a nap.

* * *

My plan was to begin from my new zero. I had Marnie to find; I needed someone—my crime-fighting partner—who would believe what I thought was going on. I had Dr. S to find. Would he be whole or the version that was essentially an ambulatory ranch for Rex? And I needed to know if Rex were, to quote the Wizard of Oz, a good witch or a bad witch. I didn't realize the third possibility until later, and I should have, because it was the next line, Dorothy's: "Why, I'm not a witch at all."

Chapter X

By the time I got all the way out of the Ag building and back to my car, my head was clear again. Not that a clear head is necessary for most of my business. I find the confused state, the "at sea," to be best in most journalistic circumstances. I work with contingencies better if I'm on my guard and confused. But being visited by Rex always seemed to leave me somehow refreshed as if the cobwebs had been swept and the furniture arranged properly. Rex left me feeling like a tidy room.

I immediately realized that my problem as an interlocutor or any kind of interviewer was the particulars of "where." You always had to meet your subject somewhere: where they felt comfortable and would spill the beans, or where the beans were themselves but the subject uncomfortable, or combinations thereof. Problem was: where is Rex? And one of the answers that came to me was that Rex was anywhere he wanted to be at any time. I could go to Dr. S and wait for Rex to show up, buy some doughnuts and set up a TV-cop stakeout. The doughnuts would be the best part of that plan.

What I could not do—as my youthful experience with the voices proved—would be to go to any sort of authority with my story: not the press, not the doctor's colleagues, not the police, not the United Nations, not Bishop Desmond Tutu, not . . . that is, not any form of what "adult" was to me as a youngster—nobody who'd roll their eyes even metaphorically, no patronizing there-there, tell-me-how-you-feel sort at all. Been there and not going back. I would avoid the white coats, the blue uniforms, and the booby-hatch professionals. I had to get Marnie back on my side.

I made a plan. I made a list of all the things in the world we had liked together: things to do or eat or do *to* or with each other or running jokes or silent winkless sighs together. All the sex things, of course. But the nether things too, the ones that make the love things possible. Cold hands, cold feet, for example. She always had one or the other and after much volunteering on my part, she simply offered them to me one at a time for warming. Cold feet in bed—the natural one. Put them right there. Yeah, like that. But as she takes her coat off and brings the cold outside into the room with her, I pull up my shirt and offer my warm belly. That was on the list.

Then the less visceral stuff. Don't ask where she's been unless she brings it up. Before Rex, BR, I had leaned away from the jealous boyfriend business of tracking her movements. AR, of course, is where I fucked everything up like some kind of psycho FBI agent of jealousy. You'd think women would like the attention of being stalked, doubted, and interrogated. Go figure. They don't. Write that down somewhere. It's true.

So I made a point of passing Marnie's apartment hoping to see the lights blaring into the night. Night after night, no blare. She was gone, and she was going to be an essential part of my plan to bring Rex under control.

Maybe not under control. What exactly did I think I wanted to do with Rex? Return him to his oatmeal bowl? Harness him for the power of good. Evil? Not my style; I had an overdeveloped conscience and would just make myself miserable. I wish I could be Lex Luthor. It just seems it would be so exhausting every day in every way to be all evil.

And then one night the lights were on. She was holding the night at bay with glorious watt after glorious watt of incandescent worship. The cathedral was alight.

My next move was to somehow be of use to her: service, volunteerism (for art), maybe just take her library books back.

Somewhere between stalking and wooing, that's where I headed. There would be time to re-woo later on I figured. I would have to keep one eye on Rex and Rex-doings as reported in the papers. I would have to interpolate or extrapolate from the wire service information. Rex cures AIDS. Rex wrecks the interstate highway system. Rex makes a deer fall in love with a Holstein—offspring TBA. I had been reading about a virus named human cytomegalovirus or HCM, aka Herpes. It's been cruising around in humans since the beginning of time apparently making bumps here, lumps there, and lesions everywhere. But more important, it seems to nod off and just go dormant until it feels like taking a walk again in any particular human being (add monkeys and other mammals by changing a few designating letters and numbers). Now I ask the rhetorical question(s), is Rex acting like a virus? (Is Mickey a mouse or a rat? Is Pluto Goofy's offspring but can't talk? Would Arthur Schopenhauer star in a rock band if he were alive today? Is there a God?) Am I asking all the wrong questions about Rex and about Marnie? Where did I go wrong? What are the other angst-filled questions I should be asking but am just too obtuse and inane to ask? Where's Kafka when you need him?

Oh, that felt good. I return to the fractals and add Brownian motion. No I don't. What lies that way? Is all this a short version of "To be or not to be" and variations on the themes. "Who would these Fardels bear?" Damn right. Who would bear what Fardels indeed? Rex is a particular pack of Fardels tied up with string.

I decide that fractals are my way back—fractals the natural point of view. That is plan A. Plan B is that Rex is a monster (unnatural) and should be destroyed, like in the movies, like in the books, like in our nightmares.

Plan A: Rex is nothing more than a fragment of an infinitely repeated segment of nature called "life." If we zoomed back from Rex, we should be able to see a much larger Rex constituting not only Rex but all the other Rexes. Reload: Rex is a design principle, and infinite iterations of this design are the stuff of life. At least that one doesn't have to have quote marks. How about this: "Rex, is that you?"

"Yes, it's me and us."

"How many of you are there?"

"Oh, and don't forget, you too. It's you, too. We are legion."

"What are your plans for us?

"The plan is the same as it always was."

"Which is . . . ?

"There hasn't been any change at all. Who would change it? What would it even be changed to?"

"You're not answering the question."

"I am too. Before asking me about a plan, what did you think "the plan" was? That's still the plan."

"Sophistry and evasion. You are a false god."

"Now you're talkin'. Among false gods I am neither the least nor the greatest."

And here the rhetoric in my head gets self-congratulatory and frankly medieval, right on the edge of thou and thee and one great shining sword. So I stop the interview.

It has occurred to me that if Rex can occupy Dr. Sewall, then he can certainly occupy me. Or Marnie. Or the robin on the lawn. Who's next, I figure, would depend on what Rex wants. Does Rex want? Yearn after things? Again I split up the logic to see how he (He) might be at work in the world. He could want dominion of all things and all time. This is the sci-fi monster scenario. But he could already occupy everything he wanted: by spore, by whatever he used on me and Dr. S, by trained mitochondria rampaging through our DNA for all I know. Talk about your omnipresent!

The other half of the split is, I think, much more in keeping with what's been going on. Rex is just playing. Maybe he's playing to find out who he is—exactly why children play. He's building a case for himself—his infinite mercy, his infinite disinterest in humans altogether. His ethereal and perfect disregard.

All this while preparing my next move. Rex could have me committed to a mental institution quite easily. I have left a trail, in my life, of significant evidence that could be used at any moment for an institutional commitment ceremony. Into the home for the bewildered. Into the booby hatch. Marnie was right. I had gone off only one of the many deep ends that are part of my tenuous self.

My only real problem is that I'm alone: Marnie is not (yet) on my side, Dr. S could be an ally if I could catch him again when Rex lets him out for a walk, and the rest of the world (including his colleagues) thinks whatever happens in the world is perfectly unconnected to an entity called Rex. Rex the crumbling brownie, the bowl of oatmeal, the spore-traveling thrill seeker. Rex the cheese, the big cheese.

So clearly, my first job is to get one more on my side.

I begin to stalk Marnie from behind trees and cars again. And, of course, since she's so much smarter than I am, she's on to me almost immediately. She sneaks up on me not a full week into my stalking period.

"And so, Mr. James." She a-has me from behind. I had been using a café down the street from the gallery to get glimpses of her coming and going. She must have come in some back door—she's known the owners for years, it turns out—and done the tip-toe to get right behind me as I sat spying out the window. She asks, "Vat is your business here? Let me zee you-r papers, pleeze."

The German accent was a longstanding shtick between us. A good sign. The next line was: "Ve-er are you-r papers—schnell!" I waited. She patted three fingers into the palm of her hand to indicate the schnell-ness of the paper demand. I reached into my back pocket, produced my wallet and gave it to her. As scripted, she riffled the contents and pronounced that they seemed to be in order. The whole thing smacked of forgiveness with each segment of our shared German-soldier-on-a-train during a WWII movie. My only problem was whether to tell her everything at once, or let slip the details little by little. I decided quickly on the incremental approach.

I was so happy to have her back, even provisionally, as she

made clear. I was not exactly on probation, but we were going to take it slowly, slowly, and that meant keeping two places to live. I had to find Dr. S also. Turned out that was easy.

* * *

On a Wednesday afternoon (Wednesday's child is full of woe), Doctor Sewall called a press conference. He also alerted the local news stations and apparently every AI and sci-fi and comic-con and computer-geek organization his assistants could find. The scene reminded me of a grand opening of a shopping center. The air was thick with commercial funk: ribbons, banners, flowers, a giant scissors, pretty girls and a display of tech gear of some sort. The press was there but not sure why. It was ado and folderol, and shenanigans all at the same time. Dr. S raised his hand for silence.

"Thank you. Thank you. Thank you everyone for coming out this afternoon for only the promise of something interesting, maybe some good news, maybe a breakthrough of some sort. I want to thank our hosts, Radio Shack, Intel Futures Division, and Netgear. Each has some part in our display of what the future holds in store."

Then he stopped talking, still holding the microphone, looking out over the crowd as if someone had pulled his plug. He stood perfectly still for a long, long time. The crowd began to make noises and shuffle as if getting ready to flee. Then just before the crowd got so restless it would break up, he suddenly began talking. More animated this time.

"And," he began again, as if he had never paused. "And each of our sponsors for today will be thoroughly displaced, their business ruined, by what I have to unveil today." He laughed, a sort of cackle and snort at once. "So be sure to dump your tech stocks on the way home. Oh look there. That guy's already doing just that from his phone. Sell. Sell. Sell!"

Several young men in the back behind the doctor began to look at each other wide-eyed. I assume they were the reps from the tech stocks the doctor was about to blow up. More phones came out. Calls being made, stocks being traded. The tapping of phone faces was audible and like the sound of a gentle wind in trees far away.

"In fact, there will be lots of tech stocks on the brink of uselessness." He shifted voice like the movements in the Gettysburg Address. "Maybe some of you oldsters remember that years ago, maybe forty or so, there was much speculative talk about what the next chip set would look like. Would it even be a chip? What was the future of memory in a larger sense? Some may recall the 'meat chip.' It would use the architecture of human DNA as memory circuits. You might sit down at your computer and spit in a slot and have all the fresh memory the computer could handle. Pretty much fun, huh?"

The crowd now was in full babble and snort. Whispering had become full on scatting at the first minutes of the apocalypse. Pharaoh's army was about to be drowned.

"The meat chip is here and its name is . . ." The doctor paused dramatically. *Rex,* I thought. *His name is Rex.* Now everyone will know.

". . . Legion. Its name is Everyman. Its name is Jean, John, Johannes, Ian, Ivan, Joan, Jeannie, Jane. . . . You, my friends, will be the new chips. You won't even have to say yes. The yes is already implied. You won't need to join up or enroll. You can't say yes and you can't say no. You will be and you will gladly be. That's the best part. No assembly required. Spread the good word. From this day forth, you will be the meat chips waking and sleeping, drunk or sober, Protestant, Catholic, Muslim or Jew. Welcome every one. Welcome home."

And suddenly I realized what was going on. Rex was going to try a group what. . . ? Invasion. Intervention. Possession.

Jake to Rex. Jake to Rex. Come in Rex. Talk to me. It's me, Jake. Make me your henchman, Rex. Let me help you. You'll need lieutenants. And commanders. And colonels. Make me a colonel, Rex. A general. Make me a general.

I had seen the power of Plan B for the world: Rex at play. No silly governments or megalomaniacal goofballs would be able to "rule" anybody for their own good. No Second Coming. The Coming will already have been. We'll all play together, and that alone will be the point—play.

The front of the crowd had backed away from Dr. Sewall. He had entered a trance again, staring over the audience as if studying something far away. He seemed to be reloading like a video with slow bandwidth. I was thinking that at any minute Plan B would be announced. But nothing came out of Dr. S's mouth. Are you there, Rex? It was as if the good doctor were taking time to re-think his rhetorical strategy. Ahem, um, in other words . . . and then he began to talk again, slower, lower, without the microphone. There appeared the sheen of sweat on his forehead and upper lip.

"I'm here today to announce a breakthrough of some significance." He clearly had begun again from some early point—reset. "What we have known as memory since the advent of the binary system has served us very well. But it has recently been holding us back too. I believe its song has finished. Zeroes and ones have always represented a rounded-off version of the actual complexity they were supposed to represent. Musicians knew this early on. Digital recordings were really only samplings of the actual sound—not the full sound itself that was available on analog recordings—pop, wow and hiss included free of charge."

The partially dispersed crowd was wandering back to hear the doctor.

"But still we shot payloads into space, photographed the heavens, mapped the human genome with our faithful servants, zero and one, giving their best approximation of the real. Now we will have the next step. Today we can reproduce the full complexity of sound, photo, any algorithm with full representation. It took something akin to the actual human brain to do it. Mathematics gave us—always—versions, representations, maps. What if you could now work with the actual city rather than a map? The actual circuits rather than the schematic diagram?"

The crowd that had reassembled was now stirring as if wafted by some unseen wind. I stood at the back and watched the crowd arrange itself, at first into lumpy groups, then very quickly into rows, phalanxes: the shuffling of feet, the squaring of shoulders. I could look down the rows now like orchard trees planted by GPS into exact lines, first this way, then also that way. I felt the need to line up at the end of one row. Very quickly, as soon as I lined up, I felt no more compulsion. I had reached the place I belonged. I was at rest. The crowd rows aligned and stopped. Dr. S smiled and paused and looked over what he had wrought.

"Can you locate yourself relative to everyone else? Imagine how useful this might be, all you meat chips lined up into the first step of real organization. On your left, you have cooperation. On your right, cooperation."

The group began to buzz. Some on the edges where it was easier to step out of line, brgan to wander then quick-step back into line, anxiety erased. Then out. Anxious. Back in. Comfortable.

"Ah, isn't that better? See how more comfortable you are when you cooperate? Thank you for your attendance today and for your . . . your cooperation. The meat chip is on its way to a device of your choice. Thank you. I will take questions at the email address on the handout. Let's chat!"

And he was gone, like the wizard disappearing back through the curtain. The crowd milled and churned and asked what had just happened. One redhead from the front row said we had imagined the lining up. One blond from the back row said no, we were definitely lined up; he could see the x-axis and the y-axis, the file, the formation, the ranks. The rows were gone instantly as perhaps a hundred people milled. There were a number of explanations circulating about what had just happened. The illusion of order is very easy, one announced. Another insisted that all order was illusion. Then the metaphysicians rose up and into the abstract gaps: we had been projections or maybe Platonic shadows of our own need for order in a world of chaos. And my instant favorite: we had for a moment all realized together that we are essentially one and all separation is the illusion.

Doctor Sewall had floated off leaving us to buzz and speculate—just what he wanted apparently.

Then came the cyber-buzz. The "chat" he promised created what became known as Yasgur's-farm syndrome. Woodstock, on Yasgur's farm, apparently held hundreds of times the number of people that it could actually hold, if one were to believe all the people who reported they were there twenty years later. Yearning to have been there counted as attendance. And why not? As with Woodstock, Dr. S's séance (as I began to call it) was not so much about actually having been there as it was about understanding or theorizing what might have gone on. In time, the full Yasgur's-farm syndrome would manifest itself, and maybe, just maybe, everybody in the state would have been there, everybody in the surrounding states, too.

Chapter XI

I needed my partner, my crime-fighting associate. Marnie. This wasn't going to be easy, I figured, and I was right. I ruled out all the madman stalker techniques I had seen in the movies. Women and men both loved attention. But crazy-person attention was not very close to the attracting kind of attention. Where to draw the line? I needed considerate and passionate without wacky and creepy. If I could do what Rex does, I'd just drop out of a tree like wafting pollen on the evening air, she'd accidentally snuff me up her nose, I'd work toward the brain—some lower centers at first, some amygdala or hippocampus—then zip on up to the frontal lobes for the reunion. Party hats. Noisemakers. There'd be cake!

But no. No such skill set, alas. She was back at work after her sabbatical to god-knows-where, so I thought I'd start there at the gallery. The fractal show was in its last week. I went there on an early afternoon, pretty casual, glance here, long look there. I knew she was in the back and could see on CCTV who as out in the gallery. She could send out one of the other girls. She could come out herself after a while. She could slip out the back door and go home for the day with a headache. She could greet me again with a German accent. She could call the police. She could . . .

"Jake," she says. "Nice to see you again. Still pondering the fractal way?"

We had talked and talked the fractal, the natural nature of the concocted algorithm of the scale of reality and the reiterative nature of the . . . that kind of love-nibble stuff, sitting on the couch our thighs touching and untouching. Me working toward licking around the rim of her ear with my pronunciation of "algorithm." It seemed like a good idea at the time, and it was. We could always morph that kind of discussion into something in the bedroom or on the couch. Then, alas, came crazy Jake and his all-jealous circus. She hated that circus. The clowns especially. Well, the main clown.

So I knew where I had to start again. With me. But I also had the sneaking suspicion that the "Me" I was going to rehab was, what. . . ? Now somehow a compounded me. A me with a tincture of Rex. A soupcon. Rex, is, I realized, running some part of my frontal lobes where the blah, blah, blah of words comes from. Was he showing off for Marnie? Was this word-jazz that started to come out of me just Rex fooling around or was it the equivalent of a twelve-year-old male doing a cartwheel for the girl over there across the playground?

Conclusion: In all the possible cases, there's not a damn thing I can do about it. So just get on with the re-courtship even if I have a passenger, a parasite, a voyeur plunked on my shoulder waiting for us to have sex so he can watch. And prime directive: don't tell Marnie about being possessed, occupied, inhabited.

Marnie cocked her head and looked at me as if looking for signs. "You've been working a lot, haven't you?" She laughed. "I can always tell when you've been stuffing yourself with research. You get that . . . that tanking-up look, like a hungry man about to eat."

"I'm just still chasing Dr. Seuss. It's kind of turned into a full-time job. The story keeps growing."

"I saw that. On the news they had footage of the event, the gathering downtown led by Dr. S. I kept looking for Horton and a Grinch. Red fish, blue fish . . ."

I have to say in the next ten minutes I found myself more charming than I ever remember myself being. Flirt charming. Eye charming. Listen charming. Oh yeah, and body contour charming, you know, the way you can shape your body to what the object of your affection is doing without touching. She concave, you convex. Rex, are you there? I wanted to call him out. Was he pushing buttons and pulling levers? Could I be this charming on my own? I finally had the distinct impression that I should break this off while it was going well, grab my laurels and run before I wreck something by overdoing or underdoing; it's such a delicate thing, this sex-schmoozing.

I think I'll check my watch as an exit move. But I can't. I mean I actually can't. Rex won't let me. In his exalted opinion I shouldn't check my watch in order to excuse myself. Well then, how about a coughing fit? A muscle cramp? A sudden case of diarrhea? Marnie is saying: "The fractal show is just about sold out. We did the 'price adjustment' thing at the end, of course. The prices became more and more negotiable there at the end, but we sold out."

I said, "I try to imagine all that math hanging on people's walls screaming squares and *n* plus ones and the coastline of England." Marnie looked at me puzzled. Well, I did it, went off some deep end. The coastline of England? Oh yeah, she'll remember. Mandelbrot pondering the actual coastline of England comes up with fractals. Something like that. "The coastline of England. Um, how that works. The ins and the outs? The bays and . . . points and projections . . . the isthmuses and the fjords . . ."

"I don't think England has fjords. But Scotland has firths, I think." She laughs.

"Does England have firths then?"

"Maybe they're the same thing."

I hear Rex gathering up his notes and making for the door of my psyche. Or maybe he had taken up residency in my soul. Where is the soul located? The thymus I'm pretty sure. I try tying my shoe and it works. Spell broken. Marnie looks at her watch and says she has to scoot.

I debrief myself at home. What was happening with Marnie? Was Rex dabbling in my love life? Fooling around? Why couldn't I look at my watch when I wanted to? Maybe I realized the move was wrong, realized in some subterranean chamber of my experience storehouse that the watch-move is always clunky. And

I was sailing along so beautifully the watch-thing would have been a fart in the elevator of my intensions. My frontal lobes were all a-tingle as if some celebrity had passed through, waved, and was gone.

I had to get a new interview with Dr. S. Somehow an interview would help me sort out the wiggles and waggles of this business.

I returned to the journalist's prime directive that secretaries know everything and can both make possible or make impossible all fruitful inquiries.

I found Dr. Sewall by applying only the first move in my secretary jujitsu. I showed up at his outer, outer office hoping to work my way in through the layers of diffusion and obfuscation to the man himself. But the secretary said just a minute before I could launch a full-scale schmooze and then said he's got a few minutes right now if you'd like to go right in. That was Plan B.

The doctor was in. He sat with his feet up on his desk, back to the door. A radio was on low, almost inaudible. Big band sound from the 40s maybe. His office seemed lit internally somehow as if actual light bulbs were not required. Every surface seemed to give off a little light so the total effect was of luminosity rather than light source.

"Let me guess," he said, without turning. "You want to know about Rex." He took his feet off the desk, turned. "There is no Rex. Not the way you knew Rex at the beginning." There is no Rex; I could only hope. But that would make my voices truly delusional, institutional, case-study-able. The office light I had studied on the way in now began to . . . hug me, caress me, maybe comfort me. Tactile light saying something like, "there, there. It's okay." A Mom of a light saying everything will be fine just wait and see. Infantalizing light.

"The bowl of oatmeal," I said.

"*Striped* bowl of oatmeal. I like to think of that as the essential Rex. He was like a cliché there at the beginning. Or maybe like a stereotype—an essentialist reduction of certain aspects of being alive. My contribution was, as I see it now, taking orders from the universe—the One."

Oh, shit, I thought. The doctor is fleeing reality after a trauma. *The One* in a conversation, in my experience, was always a bad sign. There wasn't really anywhere to go after *The One*. Phenomenology gone feral.

But he seemed to sense my unease, my dis-ease. "Jacob. May I call you Jacob?"

"Jake. My sister calls me Jacob."

"Okay, Jake. Let me begin with the event the other day, the gathering."

"And forced march—"

"Am I going to get to talk? I thought that interviews were about . . ."

"Yes, of course, Doctor Sewall. Please." I offered my open hand as capitulation to his story. "You first. I'll ask questions later."

"I'm sure you will. So Jake, do you know how jasmine smells wafting across an evening garden? But if you get close to the jasmine flower the smell is overwhelming, actually pretty stinky. There's kind of a principle here about beauty in nature—sunsets, jasmine—don't get close. So—and I'm only just pretty sure about this—Rex has morphed into beauty, or some kind of principle of beauty. Don't misunderstand me. Rex is not beauty itself. That would be an easy mistake to make. Maybe better put is that Rex has become beautiful. And playful. Maybe childlike, but not childish. Above all, there will be no interview with Rex, if that was part of your plan. An interview of any sort is quite impossible at this point."

"At this point?"

"Please, let me try to get this all out the best I can." I nodded. It was hard not to jump in for clarification, but I would be the first to admit the load of prejudice I was carrying by now would have constricted the conversation badly. I still felt Rex as a tingle in my frontal lobes, a ringing in my fillings. It was hard to let go of that invaded feeling, not to mention all those alien-invasion movies that rattled around in my youth. The doctor continued. "It became clear to me early on that Rex was not . . . what? Not stable. Not going to be the same thing the next day. The stripes were the first indication. Why stripes? Why not polka dots? Why not little stars and moons as decoration? And the answer became clear eventually. Any of those were just as possible as the stripes. And then when the stripes were done—well, you saw the crumbled-brownie thing he left behind when he began to travel. Maybe travel is not the right word. When he began to be ubiquitous. When Rex went everywhere, then he became nowhere. Okay, better said is that Rex went out of the stripes and never came back. The event the other day? That was some part of Rex that didn't even need the rest of Rex, wherever else he was. He is now the wind, maybe. He is now the jungle and the desert, the ocean and the . . ."

He stopped and scratched his head then abruptly sat down. He slumped into a kind of defeated gray mass, the kind I saw giving the paper at the conference when I first met him. I raised my hand as if I were a student in class. He nodded.

"Maybe he's dead. Or gone. Or on vacation?"

"Nice try. I even thought that for a short while. But the event and the lining up and the rows and structure—all that was Rex back showing off."

"And is there a defense of some sort?"

"Defense! You're not getting the picture, are you? Defense? What would you defend yourself against? What could we do? We could outlaw horsing around. That'd be a place to start because that's what Rex does mostly—horsing around. Then maybe we could hit the playgrounds with a whip in hand and outlaw fooling around, play in specific and general. Can't you see that Rex has found a home in what we are, or at least what we are when we are young. Or in lots of cases old, too."

Shit, I was thinking. It's very cool in lots of ways what Rex has become. But in lots of other ways it scares the shit out of me if it's true. "So what do we do?"

"Do? We don't *do* anything. We can't *do* anything. If you wanted to conquer some other tribe, the most effective way would be to marry them and breed them into yourself. The Vikings, Alexander the Great's men both practiced fuck-diplomacy. Fuck everything that moves and then on your way back through town in a few years later you get a daddy's welcome. The Normans in twelfth-century Ireland even brought their own roosters with them and killed and ate the local roosters. When they came back, they came back to eat their own chickens."

It was the Norman chickens that made me suddenly wonder if I was interviewing the doctor or Rex. Was he—either one—just making shit up now? That would qualify as play, I guess. I looked closely at his eyes as he raved on to see if there were signs of possession. I found myself wishing Marnie were here so we could sit down afterward and parse this whole speech, discuss nuances of sanity. The Marx brothers "sanity clause" occurred to me. "Everybody knows there's no sanity clause," Chico says. Marnie would know what to look for. I spent so much time with fringy people that the weird came to seem perfectly normal. Marnie worked with artists who were actually much saner than the general population, she claimed. They were focused and passionate and really predictable after you got to know them. I was working through Dr. S's proposition that Rex was everywhere now and so was actually nowhere. Omniscient, omnipotent, OM Shanti OM. Namu Myoho Renge Kyo. The Lotus Sutra. The Lord's Prayer. The inevitable call to worship in all cultures, the call from somewhere to everywhere. To nowhere. To leave our puny selves and go out into the . . . into the . . . into the . . .

Dr. S was winding up. "Jake, there are, of course, so many ways of looking at Rex at this point. I've just tried to suggest a few. He was one thing and now, alas, I don't exactly know what he's become. Or where. So you see your question about defending ourselves, it's absurd. Nothing wrong with the absurd, but as a man of science I don't do absurd. I do paradox. I do theories in contention. I even do the discursive and the seemingly impossible that's yet to be explained. Schrödinger's cat, Kekule's dream of a snake with its tail in its mouth."

And then Dr. Sewall sighed from somewhere deep inside, the sigh not of resignation but of capitulation. He had, it seemed, exhausted for the present, all words that might explain what had been Rex and had become something more disparate and ethereal. Some transmigration of soul-lessness. I'd be sure to use that phrase in my article eventually. I wrote it on my notepad. The doctor had paused but also closed his eyes and was maybe asleep. I left quietly.

Chapter XII

The way a finch moves along a branch identifies it. The way a tree sways tells us which way the wind is blowing. The waves on the sand tell the tide. I was trying to know and then tell people about something that was true for only me and Dr. S. If just the two of us had any handle on Rex, any handle whatsoever, we would develop a shorthand, a code that only we could really understand. And we were doomed to only blither into the void and nod to each other. On the other hand, was the distinct possibility that Dr. S and I should just shut the fuck up. Take his last sigh and call it good. Wait to see if Rex rained down out of the heavens on us or decided to wipe out humanity (playfully, of course) or just for the hell of it, cure cancer. Could go either way. Wait for the signs. Watch the heavens. Eviscerate a few birds and read the entrails. Pray for guidance. Set up a flow chart. Do the hokey-pokey and you turn yourself around . . .

Marnie became a necessary adjunct, a guidepost before I slipped off into Dr. S land.

It was the evenings when I found myself most likely to encounter signs of Rex, so I tried to stick to days outside. The evenings became full of variations on the natural that I had to impute to Rex or Rex-like concoctions of my own brain. I think it was the fading light that invited all kinds of fancied versions of the real. The streetlights when they first ignited themselves hummed and emitted partial spectrum light that carved the weird into the waiting world. The blue-green light transitioning to a tired orange then the full on blare that kept the night at bay. I would walk under the lights and many times one would go out. Or it would restart, so that I began to think I was doing it. I took to waving my hand at the light, then a step and it would go out. Sometimes not. But just enough times the light would falter, stop, start again from the blue-green and work its way up again. Just beyond the light, everything was possible.

Things rustled and went bump. Things scurried and scuttled all rat-faced and whiskery in the duff. And though Rex had no fear of the limelight apparently, I think he lived mostly there in the shadow world, smelling of loam and half rot. That's where stuff was getting done, I figured. That's where Rex was most Rex.

When only the streetlights blew back the dark, there was a kind of standoff peace. I went inside to celebrate the standoff.

Marnie answered my phone call. Good first step. She agreed to a sort of date where we could talk and re-take a beachhead or two. Late afternoon and public and at a place known for its bean soup. Who could not be amenable while eating bean soup?

We could meet and eat, I figured, and then plan our response to Rex, and if there was no response possible, we'd find a cave somewhere to wait out the apocalypse engineered by unattenuated "horseplay." I needed her good counsel on the subject of Dr. S, too. She had good sense. I had some sense but not much of it good. I was an enthusiastic bumbler of sorts and my only really fine quality was that I knew it. I knew it, and I knew what kind of trouble that kind of bumbling could get me. I knew to ask for help from the sensible people around me.

And yet she arrived wearing a Judas Priest T-shirt. A sign, if I were to begin collecting signs and assembling them into a message from the fractured world. What would the next sign be? And the next? Marnie brought news.

She had been cutting out articles for me from the *New York Times*. One I already knew about was on a cytomegalovirus. She thought I'd like the name alone. The fact that it was part of the herpes family was just frosting. She brought one about a sea snail, a nudibranch, that ate algae and then kept the algae alive in its gut and used the algae's ability to photosynthesize as a food source for itself. It actually kept the algae alive in its gut longer than the algae would normally live. Ka-ching! She knew that kind of stuff perked up my ears, snatched my attention, and also rang my bell, etcetera, etcetera, etcetera (as the King of Siam was fond of saying).

Was this kind of information admissible evidence regarding the whereabouts of Rex? Of course *I* thought it was. But one of the many reasons I wanted Marnie back was the good proportion she would provide my tendency to wickedness and my fondness for all partial evidence. She would say: I don't think so. And she'd say: wait just a minute or let's look at this closely and slowly. Or she'd fold her arms across her chest and say nothing but raise her eyebrows to get me to reconsider my half-cocked suppositions. She could make me reconsider, after a while, by merely raising one eyebrow.

I valued her as a human being more fully evolved than I. If Rex ever became wise, he would use her as a model for where humans should go next on the evolutionary scale. I'd take it up with him next chance.

The bean soup came and was beautiful. Marnie ate with the light coming through the window as if it wanted a taste of soup from her lips. She sipped. And the light sipped with her. I could tell she was trying to get a feeling for the degree of my wackiness, how far back I might have to come in order to qualify again as a boyfriend. At least I think that was the verbal dance we were doing. I was taken in by the light both on her and emanating from her. And, of course, after a very short while I had that oh-shit feeling of Rex's presence, the same light-presence I'd seen coming off Dr. S.

She said, "You're looking well. All this Dr. S business doesn't seem to have kept you from sleeping."

Then it occurred to me that *I* might also be putting out some light of my own. That would be so like Rex: *Hmm, what if I turned them both up a few watts, just for the duration of the bean soup? Then I'll make her lick her lips just a little, yes, like that, and then he'll blush but won't be able to take his eyes off her lips and then a truck will go past and the sunlight coming in the window will flash off and then back on so that she flickers in his eyes like a chimera that comes and goes and comes back. Then she watches him sit up straight in his chair, stretch a little, and she notices how the fabric of his shirt clings to his chest. He hasn't been working out, but I'll make it look like he has. Let's see. Which one should I have stand up and have to pee. The other one will watch and see how the body moves, catch the walk, remember the day when they lay on the quilt . . .*

All it took was the first shove and the boat of my imagination scooted out into the current and was on its way downstream and toward the waterfall. I was listening to her but multitasking my way into a parallel scenario. I can repeat everything she said—the sales of the fractals, the next show and the troubles with one painter not getting paintings done on time, the bosses taking off for Barbados, the wall repaint, and the inquiries about the Event with Dr. S. But some kind of Rex business was afoot, too.

I tried to lay out for Marnie what I thought constituted some kind of presence of Rex, or maybe the Rex principle now that Himself no longer actually appears. Told her about the "interview" when he spoke to me seemingly using my teeth as transmitters. That would be my first clue in a list of clues—that feeling. Then there was the "event" business where I knew he was afoot by the behavior of others—people, yes, but maybe birds and dogs and cats too. Then the glow thing—Dr. S's posture and attitude, my own glib silver-tongued transformation. The newspaper articles that chronicled Rex abroad in the world: mutations, irregularities, atypicality, flora and fauna surprises. I asked Marnie to add to my list.

"Fractals," she volunteered. And then she sat back and looked so beautifully smug as if she'd said all there was to say. And then finally, "Fractals and fresh-baked bread. Fractals and when the bean soup is truly fine bean soup. You know, when the whatever gets to be *great* whatever: sunset, sex, rain running down a window. The times when these are the really fine versions of the regular versions that we don't pay much mind. I mean who ever knows when sex is going to do that thing it does when you sort of black out from the fierceness of the climax. Is it Tuesdays? Four in the afternoon? No . . ." And she paused and raised her indicating finger to indicate, "It's Rex. In residence. At home. Keeping promises!"

I sat back and admired. The old fun, the new fun she was. She was being deliciously silly, but she was also onto something, maybe a Rex-tenet. Who could ever explain the variations and waverings in the fragile surface of the world?

We sat and talked and talked. That simple. After Rex we returned to art, then journalism, then, finally, us—partners in crime fighting again. We'd give it a try. No crazies allowed.

After the furniture moving (or returning), the bookshelves restocked, the kitchen cleaned, the closet organized again, we sat with the paper in the morning and saw that it had actually begun—Rex was manifesting everywhere at once.

At first, it was the same science stuff that we'd been seeing: new species of millipedes, a toxic orchid, a nudibranch with new skills. Same old same old. But also an estimated hundred thousand people in Bangladesh assembled on a beach to watch a particularly spectacular sunset, and then after light had gone, most stayed well into the night singing and praying for no particular reason—no holiday, no festival. Religions mixed, customs flowed into each other without conflict. Some kind of weird peace had broken out. No one killed in a bridge stampede. Just an orderly recession back to where they had come from. There was great public puzzling and questioning the next day about what had actually happened. Clerics railed against "mixing" prayers. Some thought they saw glowing lights.

I read the article to Marnie. She plotted it on her evidence chart that we both began to call, the "manifestations." We plotted all the manifestations of Rex and order of certainty: pretty sure, a bunch that weren't, ones that were actually our presumptive assigning of points where and when we assumed the world was being Rexed. We had a verb. We had plot points enough so that if we stood back from the chart, we observed a kind of dust effect at particular locations on the map. It made me want to connect the dots and see what duck or puppy appeared. But alas there were no numbers, no place to begin or end. You could connect the dots any way you wanted.

We could have gone on like this, Marnie and I, playing and collecting and supposing and seriously fooling around. But one day I saw on her phone—I was snooping, I admit it—the digital residue of a recent call from Dr. S. I recognized the number immediately. Since she hadn't said anything about the call and I couldn't bring it up without re-qualifying as the crazy, jealous shit who suspected everyone and everything, I was stalled in my conflicted tracks. Among my people we have a saying for when no reasonable thing can be said: "shit and two are four." I have always thought the saying got more and more useful the older I became, and I looked forward to the time as an old man when I would use it ten or fifteen times a day just to contain my dismay.

Oh, Marnie. Oh, Marnie. *Et tu*?

I thought the best thing to do in the short term was get out of the house, walk and walk. And walk. I headed toward my favorite park with its parcel of woods and pond, my refuge in the past. But on the way there I realized that if Rex was actually capable of being everywhere, messing with the world like a willful child, then there was no refuge. Maybe I should re-examine what I meant by refuge in the first place. There was no refuge from getting a cold. No refuge from twisted ankles, chapped lips, a stye, hemorrhoids, cancer—but I digress. No refuge, that was the important point. From bad luck, too. What the hell did I think I could do? I had read the Book of Revelation: run to the mountains, run to the sea—doesn't matter because you can't hide. Not from the apocalypse, not from Rex.

Of course Dr. S and Marnie were in cahoots, but what kind of cahoots? And there it is—the cahoots principle. All things, all people, all winds fair or foul were in cahoots. My personal 20 percent discount—reduce the threat level at least 20 percent all the time—was designed by me for my own protection. Because if there were no discount, the world would be unlivable—too much collusion, too much cahoots, too much crazy. Wouldn't get anything done. I'd be swatting away at all the flies, all the gnats and no-see-ums, all the things that want to fly up my nose or lay eggs in my brain—the certain plot that dirt has, to bring me on down and eat me up.

I found my cottonwood trees. These wrinkled beasts that ate up the dirt, these hanging trees of the Old West, not because they were particularly good for hanging someone, but because you couldn't find a decent oak for miles, and there was always a cottonwood right over there. They stood in a row as if planted fifty years ago by some lover of their artificial snowstorm every spring, their cotton drifting and floating and looking to make the world into one big cottonwood farm. The bark was rich gray with deep crevasses adding black shadow so that as you stepped away, the trunk shimmered. And like teenagers, the trees scattered detritus around as if claiming space by pure dint of chaos.

And just beyond their untidiness was the pond, and if I was early, and if I was quiet, and if I was lucky, a box turtle would be sunning itself on the end of a log sticking out into the water. Turtles are always wary, of coyotes I supposed; if I came on too fast, it would one-step into the pond. Today, there were two turtles lined up like solar arrays processing the sun. I got close. Each was trusting the other to bolt first. Had Rex tried out the mind of a turtle? I certainly would if I could. It would be fun to feel the sun starting up my engines ray by ray, feel the torpor slough out of my limbs, my brain kick into warm mode then plunge myself back into the dark pond to feed. I watched the two turtles tanking up on sunlight. They seemed asleep until behind me a dog wallowed into the woods looking for a drink at the pond. I turned to check the dog, looked back, and the turtles were gone. There were no ripples on the pond. I asked myself if the turtles were actually there and decided that the question itself belonged in the 20 percent cause/effect discount rate the world deserved. *I* deserved.

I spent the afternoon shifting around the park asking myself Thoreau-like questions: what does the thin layer of the natural world mean to tell us about being alive in it? What does the next layer deeper want to give us as metaphor? And then, once again, the Tina Turner question: *what's love got to do with it*? I found a hotdog vendor at the far end of the park and was tempted to ask him to "make me one with everything." Marnie and I loved that joke and contrived to use it whenever possible. We supposed that hotdog vendors all over the world were tired of it, but we did it anyway. Eventually cottonwood, turtle, dog, pond, hotdog slowly relieved my brain congestion, self-doubt, cosmic angst.

Only the Dr. S conspiracy remained. Why would he call her and why would that call not be part of our conversation after we had . . . we had made . . . we had what? There was, apparently, no after. Mend the thing slowly. Back the hell off, I reminded myself.

But I found at home a message on my phone from Dr. Sewall. Have to see you, he texted. Come at once.

I found him retreated to the inner most chamber of his offices. He had one leg up under himself on the chair as he often did in the early days. He looked like a worried man.

"Out the window," he said, without looking up himself. I went to his window. There was a fishpond in a courtyard, benches around, stonework, scattered students.

"What am I looking for?"

"The pond, look at the fish."

The goldfish were clearly visible even from this height. They had arrayed themselves in a perfect circle in increasing and then decreasing size. What are the chances? They seemed to be vaguely in motion, maybe feeding on something, some insect life on the surface.

"The fish? The circle of fish?"

"Yes but look closer, over to the right. In the shadows."

I saw a small, redheaded man standing as if he had just stepped out of the bushes near the pond. He seemed to be conducting as if he had an orchestra in front of him, an invisible orchestra. But the beat was slow, very slow. Up, down, up, down. And the fish slowly circled clockwise first, then reversed direction. I had to watch for some minutes to see the whole business because it was so slow. I could see now that the man had a red goatee and was wearing a heavy leather belt with a big buckle. A troll, I thought. A leprechaun maybe. A musical troll! A ringmaster leprechaun. There was something beautiful and fascinating about it. I couldn't look away.

"It's beautiful," I said slowly, to myself more than to the doctor. "That guy . . . who is that guy?"

When he didn't reply, I looked over at him, and he shrugged. Then shrugged again. Finally he said, "Some guy. It doesn't matter—"

I interrupted. "But he looks like a leprechaun. Or a troll or something."

"It doesn't matter." Dr. S sounded defeated. I was almost giddy with the show going on out the window. "It doesn't matter because every day it's somebody different. I've been watching all week. Sometimes a coed, sometimes just a kid passing through with his skateboard. One time a very big dog—I don't know what kind of dog is that big—just sat where the guy is today, just sat there and didn't move and the fish did the same thing . . . their ballet or whatever it is. Then pretty soon a guy calls the dog and the dog runs off and the ballet stops." Then the doctor fell silent again and sighed.

"Rex?"

"Rex. Of course, Rex."

"How can you be sure it's Rex?"

"It's the same business as the event at the mall. Make some weird order and then stop. Then do it again. Like he was just playing with something, but we can't see the toy, just what happens in the world, what gets manipulated. You think it's beautiful? Bullshit. It's not. It's just the preliminaries to some really bad stuff coming up. This is the dress rehearsal, Jake. The play opening out of town."

"Or," I offered hoping to spin this a more positive way, "Or Rex, is just exercising new muscles. Working out. Finding his way. Learning his song."

"You can't be that stupid. You've seen enough by now, haven't you? This is not a person in any sense of the word. This is a . . . a principle working its way out in the world. It's a perfectly natural principle, and it frankly doesn't give one shit about us or anything else. It doesn't have the giving-a-shit capacity. It doesn't need that capacity for anything it's doing."

I looked back out the window. A few people had gathered around the pond to watch the fish perform. They were calling to friends to come look. The small man conducting took a step back slowly and disappeared into the bushes. I noticed that his clothing was the same green hue as the bushes, and he fit perfectly into the height of the shrubs. Then the fish swam off randomly.

"It's over. It's done I think."

Dr. Sewall laughed his kind of cackle, sort of an unpleasant sound. A laugh of no charm whatsoever. "It's not done. Not by a long shot. It's barely begun. This has been happening every day for a week. Next week? What? You think this display is cute. Beautiful, you said. It's dangerous, I'm trying to tell you. It's an escalation of the level of competence. Maybe competence is the wrong word. Level of . . . of . . . potency. That's it. We're talking about power. A level of power that's just beginning." He put his head in his hands.

I wondered if I should finish off his despair with the chart

Marnie and I were keeping: the nudibranchs, the orchids, the German autobahn disasters. Should I tell him: You have no idea, Dr. S, how far this has gone beyond the fishpond. And how the fishpond and any number of simultaneous events could be going on while Rex was also fooling around in the realms of human passion? No give-a-shit capacity? *Au contraire,* doctor. Rex had become a bundle of giving a shit, but that bundle just didn't match up with what *we* happened to give a shit about. And probably never would. So, dangerous? Absolutely. But also absolutely nothing to be done about it except to dance the dance that was coming up. By my estimation the dance was just as likely to be delightful as it was to be horrible. And maybe the in-between also had a good chance: a little of everything.

Instead I told the doctor my take on the evolution of Rex, how he had gone out of the barn—literally—a long time ago, probably riding a sheep fleece like Ulysses or a load of manure the first time. He had gone toward the light out of the dingy barn and never really come back. Now what should we do about it? I reminded him of the Africanized bees that escaped an experimental genetic cross in South America. Couldn't get the bees back into the tipped over hive. Accidents happen. Shit happens. There you are. Whatareyougonnado?

"It was always thus," I pronounced biblically, waving away apocalypse. I felt as if I had lifted a burden from the doctor's shoulders. From his look, I clearly hadn't.

He said slowly, "Don't you see? *I* did this. I am responsible. This is on me. Rex is toxic. Is *going to be toxic* because he can't be otherwise. Because he will because he can. Be toxic. Jake. We will soon be in the woe-is-me phase, I'm afraid. Some old prophecy come true to smite the wicked. Or we'll think we were wicked, anyway."

"Smiting and wickedness? Really?" It was, of course, my fault for introducing the biblical "thus." My fault entirely. The doctor was on the edge and going over.

"Yes. All those metaphors for our nincompoopery, our inability to be good. Even the most obvious good—don't hurt people, don't hit children, don't be mean. We couldn't even do that. And then I made this thing out of zeroes and ones that will kick our asses whenever it wants to. It's just warming up for the kicking, Jake. No mistake about it. Some kind of bible smiting is right around the corner."

There was no consolation for the doctor. He was slipping off into the land of Job's wife and Eeyore. Throw up your hands, curse God and die, expect the worst. A sort of evil end-of-times with a few dog bites and nasty rashes first. And then the big ka-boom, the opposite of the big bang, as Rex undoes all creation.

At least this was how I saw the doctor's mind, his doomsday choiring of the filthy dusk of humankind. That phrase actually occurred to me. I wrote it down, looked it over, thought through the alternatives to it, crossed it out, wrote it again. Smiled. Goddamn it. It was Rex. It had to be. Knocking on my doors, crying at my windows. Damn it and damn it. The doctor was wrong. No Ka-boom. And also no whimper. No bang, no whimper. Just a bowl of oatmeal fucking with the kingdoms and orders and phyla and . . . the classes. Don't forget fucking with the classes. I knew when I was amusing myself furtively like this that Rex was close by if not in residence. This is where the voices come in, but this time I heard only "hypotenuse." It was like ordering a pizza. Someone called me up and instead of *pizza* gurgled the word *hypotenuse*. A first time for that word, but not for just a word, any random word occurring to me as if from a voice. But we've been through all that before.

I needed Marnie. She would be my graph paper, my structure and reference. My x- and y-axes.

I left Dr. Sewall grousing in his office about the form the end would take. He continued to insist that wrack would follow ruin and dem bones might not even rise again. There was no talking him into a more pleasant scenario. He seemed utterly defeated—a husk.

* * *

By the time I found Marnie it was late afternoon, the hour, I had come to realize, that Rex loved for making himself manifest. I had also come to think of his appearances as unfolding of immanence. I also realized that I couldn't just sit by passively; I had to look. And I wasn't disappointed.

There he was in full possession of Marnie as she saw me out the gallery window and rushed out to greet me. She hugged me with her whole body, almost lifted me off the ground. Kissed me. But I knew she was supercharged by Rex. He was fooling around, finding out, I suppose, how it felt to be emotionally human, sexy, in love (I hoped) and thoroughly female. I could feel her nipples through my shirt as the hug lingered.

I had already thought through the consequences of Rex doing an afternoon unfolding in both of us at the same time; I expected it, looked forward to it. But I didn't feel that frontal lobe thing he did to me, the thing that resulted in me writing "the doomsday choiring of the filthy dusk of humankind." No silver plating of me. No extra charge. But Marnie was on fire.

She burbled about the new show, how she had eaten some kind of tuna salad for lunch at the little café, you know the one, that had dried cranberries, walnuts and tarragon in it and one more thing, or maybe a couple of things that made it taste vaguely Middle Eastern and it was easily the finest of all tuna salads on earth. She pointed out to me how fine I was looking in the shirt she had given me two years ago, how I filled it out better now than I did when she first bought it.

Hi Rex, I wanted to say, but didn't. Thanks for the ego licks, the self-esteem snuffs, the strokes. But thanks most of all for the hug, the nipples, the way the whole afternoon light shifts spectrum and begins to include a couple wave lengths up there on the red end that we rarely get to see. And good work on the blue end, too. Some kind of filling in, fleshing out. Hi Rex.

Of course, I never said a word to Marnie and was still plotting how exactly to bring up this peripatetic multitasking Rex was doing. How would I ask her to help me plan for some negative possibilities suggested by Dr. S while she was high on Rex juice? And then she whispered in my ear that she could get off early and we might, just might, like to spend all the rest of the afternoon making love and not put on clothes until a late dinner at the Italian place we loved. You know, she said, just to keep our strength up.

And when we got home and began throwing clothes here and there, put on the music, I felt him too. He was going to make love to himself. Rex on Rex. I knew immediately that I would do exactly the same thing if I were Rex. The possession was gentle and joyful at first but then fierce and funny, and for a second I wondered what he would do with the rising feeling, that hormonal fire, the blood heat. Maybe he'd try flowing back and forth between us, going male to female to male to female again and again. Or just do both at the same time like a god-ride for Tiresias.

We took out the peaches Marnie had brought home the day before. There would be a lot of laundry to do later. We slurped and ate the peaches off every surface the human body would allow peaches. Somehow the peaches that weren't near ripe the day before suddenly became fully peach-soft ripe and juicy.

She tied one of my hands to headboard but left the other one free to touch. The peaches couldn't stay inside their skins; we couldn't stay in ours. The afternoon light reddened with peach and the world was a single and full-throated yes. Yes. Yes.

Even afterward, the lingering waves of feeling stayed on beyond nature's regular way of saying, "well done." We were both caught in a flood that wouldn't let our nerves return to the business of the world. I couldn't actually do anything that resembled thinking. Rex was trying out some variations on both of us; we could clearly remember and were fully stuck in the climax. It didn't go away. We could remember it like a phone number or where we'd left the car keys. We lay tasting and re-tasting the entire climax. Both of them.

I looked over at Marnie and saw she was as thoroughly idiot-brained as I was. Rex has fucked us both. No, that's not the right way to say it. He had used us both at the same time to fuck. . . . Not that either. He *was* both our climaxes and then he gave us the gift of remembering them. Not even that. It was just such a hell of thing all together.

So we went again, came again, played again and again until the Rex principle had had enough. I fell asleep and slept, I don't know how long. I awoke to Marnie sitting upright in bed with her legs crossed staring at me like Venus in that Botticelli painting of Venus and Mars where Mars is spent and asleep, Venus awake with desire and four satyrs playing with a phallic wakeup call. Let's do that again, the whole picture says. Marnie needed only that Venus braid that binds her out into nature with her yearning. Marnie was yearning.

But apparently Rex had left me while lingering in Marnie. Only way I can say it. I was left washed up on the beach, Marnie still afloat.

There were peaches and peach parts everywhere. A more thorough stickiness would be hard to imagine. Both nooks and crannies were sticky. Hills, dales, glens, vales—that's the idea. We were a landscape of laundry nightmare. But clearly, the laundry strategy was only occurring to me, not Marnie. I tried. I tried but kept falling asleep as if Rex had decided to stand on my eyelids just to see what Marnie would do about it. Maybe asleep is not the right word. I was nearly devoid of words. Drugged: that's close.

When I awoke again, Marnie was sleeping next to me; we were covered and stuck to every inch of the sheets. Rex must have grown tired of the experiment and left us both on the beach finally. And as I came to, I began to wonder just what he found out. Did he discover the fundamental urge? The Urge that ran the human lust machine? How we all got here two hundred thousand years later? Did he get a peek at the thing itself? The great want-to?

I realized as I woke up more that I was making the Dr. S mistake. I was guessing that Rex had all kinds of complicated reasons, threads of reason beyond our poor comprehension, for exploring the world. And then all would go horribly wrong and we'd be plunged into the toxic undoing of all we had known of the world. Wrong Dr. S. I was going to stay with Rex-at-play. He wanted (I know I would, just like with the turtle) to feel it. Feel how good it feels. There would be no more perfect thing a god could do than just use people to feel the pleasure of being alive, ring those delight-bells over and over until the fragile metal began to crack and the great bells flew off over the horizon. . . . But I begin to Rex-up my own language. Wait a minute. I sat up in bed and became aware just how puny the human pleasure centers are compared to the pain we can endure. Pleasure just wears out, and we have to wait for the nerves to restock. But pain can go on day after day like a sere sourness that never relents or burns itself out. This pain is what Dr. S saw as inevitable in his monster. Rex would need to use people to see what pain, ineffable pain, would feel like. He'd need more than an afternoon and peaches to find that out. I think it was there in a bed sticky with peaches that I realized I had chosen the playful and juicy and delightful and lovely Rex over the painful and mean and toxic Rex. And it was really only a choice. Maybe just my own temperament imposed on Rex-ness. He couldn't just plague us just to watch us die and then walk away. He could. He wouldn't. Why set whatever zombie-apocalypse upon us in whatever form that could take—bacteria, virus, the undead—when we were much more fun slathered in peach juice lapping at each other's pleasure parts? Maybe the Old Testament God would plague and flood and burn us to keep us in line. Not Rex. Not MY Rex.

The light was gone. We showered, gathered up the sheets for the laundry, and went to eat Italian. I had osso bucco; Marnie pasta primavera, just like Venus would have.

Chapter XIII

I heard from Dr. Sewall that he wanted to kill Rex. He detailed his plan to undo what he thought he had done—sort of an anti-bowl of oatmeal. He wrote on email that he couldn't lay out the entire scheme because Rex would be reading his email. He also said that he had begun lining a baseball cap with tin foil so that Rex could not get into his head when he had his defenses down. "Defenses? What defenses?" I wrote back. "I have defenses," he shot back. We will all need defenses soon. Rex will come soon."

Shit, I thought self-indulgently. I do believe Rex may have had all the coming he can handle for a while. He's got to try out being an owl or something else now. Swooping down through the evening and scooping up a tasty mouse for his young. That's got to be nearly as good: warm meat, filling the scheme of nurturing progeny. I began to think Dr. S may be the bigger problem if he cranked up his algorithmic genius to produce a counter-force to the playful Rex. What slab of heated breakfast cereal is slouching toward Bethlehem to be born? Etcetera.

Marnie was no worse for the wear the next day, the day after what I began to refer as the Great Peach Exaltation. The GPE now lay between us as a new standard in our relationship. We could refer to it without, we agreed, trying in vain to reproduce it. We could see it over there as an historical event without being bullied by its magnificence. We did now have ants in our bedroom where there had never been ants before. Be more careful with the peaches next time—that was the lesson.

Marnie and I discussed what to do about Dr. S. Was he the danger? Was she on the same page with me about Rex?

Turned out she imputed much less, okay, none, of our afternoon delight to Rex. We were indeed on very different pages. She was all for a rational explanation: very fine make-up sex. We had stored up our . . . affection for each other and lavished it on a single extended hoo-ha of an afternoon. I thought I could let it go at that. I should have let it go at that. I didn't.

"So . . . that was great stuff yesterday afternoon. Knocked *my* socks off, anyway." I should have stopped right there. Didn't.

"Yeah," she said. "Socks everywhere. Plenty of socks for sure. Oh, did you pick up the dry cleaning. I think they were going to close early for some holiday I didn't recognize." Marnie sorted through the mail. "Bill, bill, bill."

"But maybe it was the afternoon light or something. It was like it would never stop. Or even slow down."

"Yeah, I love it when that happens."

"Oh, well, that really never happens for me. Not like that. Not to be too cheesy about it, but did you do some kind of extra mojo thing? Just asking so you might do it again if I'm really nice to you."

"Regular mojo." She laughed. "On the other hand, define 'really nice.' Maybe I will admit to some special secret thing only I know how to do. It's . . ." She was not going the direction I'd hoped for. But a nice direction, anyway. "It's really not a thing I can show you. It's, well, an internal thing, if you know what I mean. You either have it or you don't. I have it."

She shuffled the bills, threw them back onto the bill tray. I tried another way toward Rex. "And a beautiful thing it is. Even if I can't see it. You made me a believer. Still, it was like there was something even more spectacular going on, don't you think? Like there was almost a . . . presence, an emanation of some sort going on. Or . . . yes, like someone else, maybe a ghost, was in the room helping us out."

She went to toss out the junk mail and turned to me. "A ghost? You mean like a real ghost? Or more like . . ." And here she gave me that over-the-shoulder look as if she were checking for signs of crazy, as if the crazy-ometer had just been turned on. "Or more like a bowl-of-oatmeal-gone-rogue kind of ghost?" She waited; I waited; I bit my lip.

"Sure. Something like that? What do you think?"

She studied me, crazy-ometer running, gathering data. "Okay. Say Rex could jump in like that. Did he 'occupy' you or me?"

This was the tipping point. I could slide out the side door. I could say whacky shit. Somewhere between the two was going to be the right way, I thought. "I was just thinking if Rex could pull off the AI event, you know, the lining people up, why wouldn't he, why *couldn't* he jump into somebody's lovemaking."

"Just a minute. So you're saying it couldn't be my special skills." And here she patted herself obscenely but with good humor too. "Couldn't be that special 'thang' that I do, huh?"

And I found myself pedaling but not going anywhere. It was a moment best defined by the elephant/down joke. How do you get down from an elephant? Ladder/goose answers. Either one. She had me where I had to go with ladder or goose. She raised her eyebrows waiting for the answer. And I went with the goose, so to speak. The fowl answer, anyway. I chickened out and said: "What I mean to say is, the whole afternoon was otherworldly. Out of this world."

She considered my position on the subject. She checked the data on the crazy recorder. She, I think, also considered whether I might have a case in the Rex-presence theory, but she didn't say it. She said, "Yeah." And then after what seemed to me to be a very long time, though I'm sure now it was not untowardly, she added, "Do you think we could get ahold of Rex? Invite him to the party sometime and see what we get? But peaches are as far as I go. I don't do oatmeal. And I don't . . . well . . . I reserve the right . . . my orifices are . . . you know. My own."

I was thinking we had no choice in the presence or absence or Rex but wisely kept it to myself. I was also thinking about where our sex life was headed if we had to ceremoniously invoke some string of zeroes and ones to come and ménage-à-trois with us. That way lies madness, clearly. But damn that was fine the way the feeling stayed and stayed and stayed as if someone left the lights on.

The following weeks we didn't even have to check the newspaper to see Rex at work. The local news without knowing it had become Rex's personal reality show. I started keeping track, submitting my findings to the jury of Marnie for vetting. Is it Rex or is it just the weirdness of the world? Rex was becoming his own GMO show: modifying, putting in, taking out, inventing new cheeses, new wine in old bottles.

And this business could have gone on a long time if not for a panicked phone call from Doctor Sewall. The gist of the call was that if we don't do something about confronting Rex soon, we will not be able to do anything about him and his evil plans. Yes, evil. He used the word *evil,* and it rang right out of the comics. Villainous evil. Two-face and wrath-of-Kahn evil. As before, I thought my best move would be to try to talk him out of his tree, onto the ground, and then sit him down on the metaphorical park bench where we could begin a sane conversation. Not this time. He was spurting and babbling and *non-compos mentis*. On the phone he sounded as if his eggs were thoroughly scrambled. Rex and not-Rex occurred to me. Which one was I dealing with?

The doctor had been moving in this direction for some time. Maybe having Rex in his brain had weakened his infrastructure, loosened his pilings so that the whole edifice of self was wobbling now. On the other hand, how stable had that building ever been? What had he written in those early lines of code that could have (accidentally?) created the ur-Rex? The Rex that then had iterated himself into the infinite complexity I now suspected—the omnipresent, omniscient. Rex not as God him-, her-, itself. But God's fingerprint, the fractal of God.

First things first: Dr. S in pursuit of his faculties and me still in pursuit of my article. These goals, it occurred to me, were in some ways incompatible. I wanted to write an article and the "crazy doctor, mad scientist" angle, though truly hackneyed, really just needed a little complexity at the edges, an angle that portrayed the doctor not as that sad dupe Frankenstein, but played up the stroke of luck in the combination of codes that made up Rex, made up in the sense of invented and also constituted. Luck as an idea seemed all over the scientific world suddenly. Cancer was, in many cases, being described as fundamentally bad luck at the cellular level. Luck was replacing chance and chaos—very sexy stuff in the past—and even Schrödinger's cat that was both alive and dead simultaneously. Apparently the dice that Einstein said God does not play at? Well . . . God does.

I thought I had Marnie back on my side, and if I could keep in check my evil, green-eyed twin, I might pull that whole love business off again. But right now, the gurgling on the phone concerned me most. I had to play catch-up with the doctor and see what could be salvaged there. There was also the possibility that he would do something so egregiously wrong that he would become the news story and any article I could write would just be a footnote to his madness and incivility.

So I went looking for him. He was, I thought, looking for Rex with malice and murder in his eye. I was looking for Dr. S looking for Rex—two moving targets. And since I had no idea where to find Rex and in fact had designated Rex as finally unfindable, I was left only with the misty trail of the doctor whom I pictured with lab coat aflap, bug-eyed with Oedipus-like rage, and somehow growing thinner and more transparent as he sniffed out the trail of Rex. I wrote that in my notebook for the article: aflap, Oedipal rage, evanescent.

I tried the usual places—the labyrinth of Dr. S's offices and his guard-dog students. I even went back to the Ag building but couldn't even find a trace of his office there; it had been assimilated into Ag purposes. Finally, I hunkered into my computer to web-search for traces. I looked for idiosyncrasies in the fabric of scientific research that might lead me in some direction he'd gone. The previous phone call was from his cell number, but I couldn't do a missing-person report quite yet and the phone-trace thing the police do. Three days was the general rule there, I thought. I briefly entertained the idea that he had been assimilated into the energy field that Rex . . . blah, blah, blah. No use going full comic book on him yet. Stay real for a while.

Marnie texted me that she thought we should just wait and he would show up; he always did in the past. I'm not sure why I thought that this time was different. He wouldn't suddenly appear in a shopping mall with the Rex-glow on him. He wouldn't be parading around in front of fawning colleagues at a conference. Something in the gurgle and snort of the phone call, the panic maybe. Something of fear and something of resignation. *Rex was out and about* was his fear. *We are all doomed* was his resignation.

His offices, his apartment, his secretaries, his teaching assistants, his lab monitors, his web presence—dead ends. I might have tried vacant lots and high grass out at the airport and overflowing creeks and high places with cement below, maybe under bridges. At this point, it seemed any place I tried was equally possible and improbable. I didn't know the why. I didn't know the what.

I went back to Marnie at the gallery. The last of fractals were gone, and a new set of abstract landscapes was up, and the landscapes were no help. The fractals with their color flash and hypnotic repetition had some kind of synchronicity with my Dr. S business. There had been a sort of subtext in the prints to the whole irony of the rise of the doctor from the Ag building footnote for AI to the toast and envy of his scientific community. And the central part of that irony was that Dr. S was only repeating the same thing over and over, that his original creation just expanded on its own: Z=Z squared + C; that's the E=MC squared of the fractal world.

Marnie was sure that waiting would work. I was for tail chasing, scrambling around, turning over rocks, kicking the shrubs to see what I scared out. She asked me to think carefully about the whole Rex thing, the way I had it sideways in my head. That's what she called it, *sideways*. She had thought about my theory that Rex was in on our lovemaking. That way lies madness. She said that too. I was being cut off at the pass. Dr. S figured it would soon be too late to intercede on behalf of the human race and bio-tragedy was just around the corner. Marnie figured we had plenty of time to go out for coffee and a scone while we waited for word from the doctor. When the middle ground between those became manifest, everything became clear. Rex spoke with thunder from his throne.

"Ladies and gentlemen," Rex would say. "I have come to talk about need: what you need, what I need. What the earth needs. There is a singularity in the affairs of humans, a moment of fracture in the equilibrium that always leads—well, *anywhere*."

This is the beginning as those of us who heard it could best reconstruct it. Since it went on and on, there was some uncertainty as to the exact words. The other complication was that I heard it and Marnie didn't. The best I could figure out later was that about half of one percent of people heard it, and the rest of humanity heard nothing. So a lot of people heard it. But the key fact was that many, many more did not. And the preponderance of evidence, as the saying goes, is that those who heard it were not *really* hearing it since so many could testify on behalf of the great and ever abiding silence. Nothing was the winner. It didn't happen.

Here's what I remember of the rest of it. First of all, it was just like the shitty PA system of the lecture hall the first time I heard Dr. S lecturing. Low-fi, at first, then better and better fi as if someone were sound-checking the universal mind. Or less than a percent of the universal mind, anyway.

Marnie and I were sitting at the café; the drinks had just arrived. I was about to over caffeinate myself in the usual manner, getting to the stage where my ambient voices mixed with the writing habit. Two sips in though, way too soon for the full mixing of voices with paragraph forming, Rex came on my receiver, whatever it was. And whatever it was, Marnie didn't have one.

I said, "Are you getting this?" She said, "Getting what?" I repeated what I was hearing: ". . . what you need, what I need. What the earth needs." She put her coffee down and gave me the look that let me know the crazy-ometer had been activated. So I held up one finger and listened, then rummaged for my notebook and began to take notes. I figured whoever else was hearing this was getting the same looks. The address was so broadly aimed at the people of earth, the children of Gaia, the spawn of cell division, the . . . I lost track of the many addresses in the voice coming over my brainpan. I figured I was not the only one getting the message. I looked around and way down the street a guy had stopped and was looking around, up and down the building front checking maybe to see where the voice was coming from. I calculated the half of one percent later on—a guess, but a good one—as the number, the *perfect* number to indict the hearers as nuts and flakes and woo-woo ghost pursuers: the fringe crazies. Perfect number to be told shut up and go about your business and let's never speak of this again.

Rex went on: ". . . a fracture in the equilibrium that leads anywhere. The need I am speaking about is strongest in those who hear me now. The ones without the need are . . . well, just let me say that they are getting inklings and intimations without the logos—the word. They too yearn but insufficiently. They also yearn palely."

So, that much I'm pretty sure about. But the voice began to outrun my ability to take notes. The rest of what follows is the gist of the voice, or should I say, The Voice?

"We are due an adjustment. We are overdue an adjustment to the wheels and wheels within the wheels that run this engine." I'm sure of the word "engine" because it was so unexpected. He called, I think, all of human history an engine. "And then there is the winding down and the winding up, both happening simultaneously. There is a collision ahead for these two, the upwelling and ebbing are going to come together instead of taking their celestial turns." I'm not very sure about this part since the language gets pretty gooey and abstract as if it were being simultaneously translated from another language. And the fact that Marnie had put down her coffee and taken out her phone and was aiming the camera at me, this didn't help me get the message straight. I wasn't even sure there was a message that I should prophet-like be taking down for my people's edification. Where the burning bush? Where the golden plates? Where the stone tablets?

Marnie's camera seemed to grow larger and larger as if my silence were becoming an art event of some sort. But the voice was very clear in my head now and overwhelmed my own alarm going off, my crazy-self alarm that required the dedicated 20 percent discount on behalf of all input into my ragged system.

Then Rex said something like: "When we need to alter the way the world works, we will. It will. The coming together will be a hopeful catastrophe. You will know both at once, and if you can need the alteration you will be at home. If you resist the iteration"—and here I can't really remember this gaseous part very well but I'll try—"resist the iteration, then just look closer and closer to see how the embrace of what always was can be yours. Yours too." Then this next part I think I got pretty well since I immediately thought of the teddy bear's picnic: If you go out in the woods today, you're in for a big surprise. If you go out in the woods today, you better wear a disguise. But Rex actually said: "You have a home in the far forest and a home in the illusions of the masks you have taught yourself to wear. The need that has led to the home and the illusion of home is the same need. Your need. My need. What you yearn for, I yearn for. I am the need inside your yearning." I'm sure I'm screwing this part up since it sounds to me like crystal-gazing glop now. But next he wound it up with the part about fathers and mothers and circle of fathering and mothering that design provided and choose the design well for (here I waited for a "thee" or "thou" from a King James version) we will be our own children. I don't know exactly what the rest was. More of the same. Marnie restarting her camera to take a longer video to record, I supposed for my commitment hearing, the loss of reason and reasonableness that occasioned my café fit. I assumed this event would be called my café fit. Or maybe spell. More old-fashioned but somehow more apt. Alas, I've had a spell. Move over Caliban, poor Caliban.

All the time—Marnie videoing, guy's head down the street pivoting to find the voice source—all this time I'm thinking "holy shit" and then "holy shit again." It occurs to me now that those two words were not a bad description of what was going on inside my head. Holy men always hear voices, don't they? And the shit part, the excrement factor was the language straight out of the lower intestine—large bowel rhetoric. Even if it were somehow true or a truth, the message had the flavor of deceit, of fraud, like some carney or a radio preacher raving into the FM night. I was clinging to my original theory about Rex, that he was always and ever just fooling around, that we were always in the presence of play.

The afternoon light in the café became a director's light with its fierce shadows and rich amber hues. Marnie stopped her movie of my madness, put down her phone, smiled as if to reassure me it all had to be done for my own good. *We'd need a record for the authorities. Therapy could be based on this footage of the patient in the throes of having a vision of some sort. Maybe he was astral traveling as he later claimed before we began the medication.* She was looking at me as if all that were on the table.

I reduced my prophylactic 20 percent by another ten just for good measure.

"So," I asked her. "Do you think it will rain?" This was our long-standing transition—out of trouble, out of boredom, out of lapsed continuity. She laughed and stopped, I think, her vigilance.

"Jake, are we going to only do this? I mean *only* do *this*?" And she swept her hand at the afternoon in general, the vision in specific. "I mean Doctor Sewall and the whole Rex thing. Why don't we go to the lake? Just wait it all out and see what happens, and then we'll have a better idea what to do. What makes sense to do, okay? I can get off for a few days while they install the rest of the new show. They know where everything has to go. And we could . . . just go."

"Let the chips fall where they may?" I was thinking to tread lightly now. And one way was to just repeat what she said in other words.

"Yeah. Like that." She took my hand and looked at me with sizzley eyes. Something cooking on the grill.

"The lake? The big one or the little one?

"The little one. With the cute cabin, and you can't see any other houses if you sit on the porch and have a drink and look at the water."

"The one where we discussed and then decided that the Oracle at Delphi if living today, would have left Delphi and come to the porch with a gin and tonic in his hand?"

"Exactly. That one. If the Oracle hasn't already booked it. We could check."

It turned out the Oracle, or someone, *had* booked it, our porch of righteous pondering. We settled for the cabin down the way that did not have the porch that screened out all the rest of humankind, but did have a porch that would have to do.

* * *

The lake was a little over ten acres, too small for motors of any size, so there was some distant put-putting but never a roar. We couldn't see who had rented our oracular porch, and, of course, they couldn't see us. We hauled in the suitcase we had stuffed with both our things. I couldn't help feeling that I should be doing something active to find the doctor, be scoping out the manifestations of Rex that were certainly all over the back pages of *The New York Times*. I don't know—preparing myself for the End of Times. New York and others.

Ever alert for signs and countersigns, even wisps of smoke or hidden embers bespeaking the conflagration's beginning—I stopped. Not that way. Try to go a different way. Sing a completely different song.

Chapter XIV

Okay. I'll mix the drinks. Marnie's on the porch scouting what there is to ponder from there. A little more gin for each one. The problem with this porch as opposed to the Oracle's porch is that this one has interference. And it's not just the sight lines that are problematic. It's the actual interference. There is some kind of broadcast competition going on. I think twice, then three times and decide not to mention this to Marnie. She's in full lake-sigh mode, letting the water-washed light in like a skipped rock. We are in different places in the same place. Our feet up on the same railing. My chair creaks; hers doesn't.

After a long silence into which enters the wind, the water, a bird I don't recognize, two birds I do (spotted towhee, Bewick's wren), my scrambling thoughts that come down out of the trees and seat themselves in an orderly fashion on park benches, and one high-flying vapor trail without sound, Marnie says, "I read that sixty tons of cosmic dust rain down on the earth through the atmosphere every day. Should be some coming down on us right now." She laughed, but I was, alas, off with the dust blowing around the world.

The dust got immediately added into my Rex formula: one bowl of binary code oatmeal plus cosmic dust filtered in through the open sides of the Ag barn, the dust lands in the bowl, the dust has in it spores that have traveled through space seeking new and fertile agar-agar . . .

"That's a lot of dust," I say. "Are you sure that's sixty tons a *day*? Could it be a month? A year?"

"A day. A day. But it gets evenly distributed. . . . Oh, oh. That'd be even cooler if it *didn't* get evenly distributed and landed in clumps, stood up, dusted itself off. . . . Wait, could dust dust itself off? Anyway, then it . . ."

"As it would have to, it would go to a secondhand store and

find some suitable duds . . ."

And we were off, gin-fueled and laughing.

"In the Seattle area it would come out of the store with Kurt Cobain duds, cast off lumberjack stuff. Grunge."

"Space grunge."

Our laughter echoed over the lake. The water picked us up and fed our words to the fish and trees. And to whomever else was sitting on a porch and gin-pondering the water.

We heard back from the water. "Is that you, Jake? Marnie? Where are you?" The water was disguising its voice in a watery echo. We looked at each other, made the big eyes of asking a question without words. Marnie whipped out a piece of paper and scrawled *"Rex?"* on it. I wagged my finger no. And then mouthed, I don't think so. I cupped my ears to say listen again."Hello?" I said. To the water, to the space dust, to the voice.

"Hello. It's me. Professor Sewall." And then someone else laughed from across the lake. "I'm right nearby," Dr. S called. "Maybe the next cabin down."

The oracle porch. Of course. I looked for him everywhere except the perfect place. He couldn't possibly have known about the perfect place, but he did. And right away I began to wonder if Rex having been in both our brains maybe gathered a few twigs and seeds in one place and dropped them in the other, sort of like a bird dog and burrs. I thought I'd look to Marnie for some steadying before proceeding. I wrote, *"Should I ask him if Rex is with him?"* No, she finger wagged. *"Let's invite him over,"* she wrote. And since I was looking for guidance I nodded yes, thinking she must have a better handle on this than I do.

We called to him that we were the next cabin south. Come over for a drink. And through the pines came Dr. S without a lab coat, without any aura, picking his way through the bracken, watching where he stepped as if navigating a minefield. He saw us, waved and made his way around to the porch.

"Well you two. You two hiding out here like me?"

I waited to see where Marnie would go with him. I deferred.

She said, "Welcome. Gin and tonic?" He nodded, and she went to fetch, leaving me to get him a chair, get his feet up on the railing.

"We usually try to rent the cabin you're in. But you beat us to it this time. How long have you been here?"

"I'm not actually here," he said, and paused. Oh shit, oh shit came to me very quickly: Teletransporting, astralplaning, cosmic-syncing . . . "That is," he continued, "I told no one at my office, left no message forwarding. I just skipped town and came here. I think I've known about this place for a long time now. It's so familiar. I like this lake, but I like it best when I have that cottage. You know, I suppose, that you can't see any other cabins from the porch. It's like you're all alone until the lake picks up a conversation and delivers it to you, of course."

"We noticed that. Are you . . . on vacation? Resting up?"

He laughed the laugh I heard in his office on the first day, a kind of kid laugh with a barking chuckle at the end. He leaned back and put his feet up on the rail. "Jake. I'm sorry about the phone call, the panic and all. I was in a kind of . . . what? A loss of information, I call it. I couldn't figure out what was going on."

"With Rex?"

"Well, with Rex. And with other things. You know when you're doing an experiment and gathering data, and then all the data crashes together on you? What I mean is, it doesn't make any sense. All you've got is numbers in columns. Well, like that. Nothing makes any sense, but you still have to go forward."

Marnie returned with three more gin lubricants.

The doctor continued. Marnie said she could hear from the kitchen. Keep going. "That's where I was, anyway. I had lots of information about Rex but none made sense. It was just . . . *information*. It didn't mean anything. It wasn't leading anywhere, you know. It was as if I got a bunch of information randomly from different experiments . . . projects. And all that info just rattled around and went nowhere. Pointed nowhere either. No trail to follow. No hypothesis. Remember GIGO?—garbage in, garbage out? Early computer days. Programmer's lament. We'd sit around with gallons of coffee writing basic code that sometimes just collapsed on itself."

I couldn't remember the doctor going on like this before. When he was Rex-occupied he always was eloquent. When he was himself, he was crabby or silly. He took a long pull on his G-and-T and continued.

"I was blaming myself for the whole Rex fiasco, of course. Thinking he had gotten completely out of hand—an inexcusable lack of standard scientific protocol on my part. You just don't do experiments with live things that can get away from you. Proper safeguards. Lab procedures. CDC precautions." He was ticking off his errors on his fingers, speaking more to the lake than to us. "But the university wouldn't give me any clean rooms or labs with proper facilities. I was just the IT guy, the AI theorist. Why would he need a lab? What, the zeroes are going to get away and infect the ones? I heard shit like that all the time. Every time I asked for a lab with some proper protections for live experiments. So it's as much their fault. . . . No it isn't. I should never have cooked up Rex without safeguards. The university has policies; I helped write them a long time ago. Policies about human subjects, policies about infectious disease, about pathogens and dangerous chemicals. My fault. The phone call. That's when you got me with the phone call. Rex had grown silent, or I thought he had. I didn't know where he was, what he was doing. I thought . . . I *feared* he would do bad things and then worse things and then even worse things. Now, I don't know why I thought he would be evil. There was no way he could be evil. He was just a string . . ." Here insert a sigh. A sigh like I hadn't ever heard in my life. We sat in silence waiting for him to go on. Instead the sigh hung in the air over the lake, maybe made its way to the oracle's porch some hundred yards away and there emptied out all the sadness and regret and loneliness of the world. We waited. And waited. I thought, what the hell, I'd take a chance coming off as crazy with Marnie. I had to.

"Professor Sewall, I have the feeling that Rex is not so much gone as dissipated. I mean gone everywhere. Or at least found a home. In fact, the home-theory is my current favorite. Do you remember how you came to know about the cabin next door? Have you ever been here before?" Marnie, in my humble opinion, pricked up her ears, but, I think, she left the crazy-ometer off.

"I can't remember. But when I went looking for a place to go, to get out of Dodge you know, I looked up the rental number for this place. I thought I remembered it from some other time. Maybe not. Why do you ask?"

"Because I think you got it from me. I think Rex rustled around in my brain, then rustled around in yours. Left traces in the wrinkles, I think." And the second gin and tonic kicked in here so I'll try to adjust for that. "Left, like burrs collected in one thicket and deposited in another. Bird dog or something." I hadn't thought this through entirely, was being chased through my own mind by wild metaphors.

"Bird dog," he said.

"Bird dog?" Marnie said.

"Yeah, but the bird part is irrelevant. Let me work on the relevance. Maybe better is that Rex's shoes picked up dust bunnies from my brain and then he wiped his feet in your . . ." Boy, this was not getting better.

"Okay," they both muttered in different ways. We get what you're talking about. Rex left traces.

"Rex left traces," I said and rattled my ice cubes. And here the doctor raised his hand like a student in class.

"Yes, Professor Sewall." I called on him and laughed.

He lowered his hand. "Not only do I know what you mean, but I have something I'd like to add if I may. And that is, he never left. And I speak for myself of course, but if you'd like to nod or something if it's also your experience, then do. Please. So I was saying, he never left. I don't think he's gone."

I thought only briefly about it and then nodded.

He continued, "Not only never left, but never will. Maybe I'm talking about permanent damage there in the occupied parts, but that might be the same thing as occupied. He left a trail. Okay, footprints." I sighed instead of nodded. "So we are both occupied in a way. Marnie, did you ever . . ."

Marnie held up her glass. "Here's to occupation. Does it count if I never say—said—anything about it? Does the . . . does the tree still fall in the forest?"

We all laughed and then fell silent. The lake fell silent too.

After a while, a while that included splashing in the shallows halfway around the lake, included a sliver of a day moon, Doctor Sewall spoke quietly. "I really don't know what I did. I am beginning to suspect that I did absolutely nothing. I wasn't even the unwitting dupe for a cosmic occurrence. That's what I thought for a while. Imagine! My arrogance extended to being the right hand of God working out the next stage in His plans for the universe." He laughed; the cackle was gone now, the tee-hee too. "I had that ole archangel feelin'—there should be a song somewhere in it. Michael with his sword driving the sinners from the garden, Ezekiel and the burning wheel, and yours truly, Albert Benedict Sewall PhD with a fist full of fractals—an historical series."

"Fractal?" Marnie asked. "How fractals?"

"Well, there was a fractal base to Rex at the beginning. It's really pretty easy to do. You just circle the zeroes and ones around four numeric bases, only make sure they only add and multiply. That's all really. Oh, and when to actually stop. They can't just keep going like real fractals. Rex had . . . what? Stop signs. At first, anyway. Stop signs to say that there could be truncation. I began to think of the truncation as shaping or just—" The doctor broke off and smiled. Then, "You see the way the light is changing, how the water is playing off the sky but can't quite catch up. Or like that . . ." He pointed. "How it goes off on its own like it has its own color palette."

We all sat and looked. The light did indeed seem to be fooling around on the surface of the lake gathering the tree colors to the sky colors. Marnie was sitting between us, all three with our feet on the rail. Marnie reached and took each of us by the hand and said nothing. The doctor, I noticed accepted her hand like a lover.

All the while she held our hands no one spoke. Then just as suddenly, she let go and put her hands in her lap. When she was holding my hand I swear for a second I felt as if Rex were about to speak over my neurons, like the first time in the doctor's Ag building office. Maybe it was only how surprising and nice it felt sitting here, the three of us. Then I thought, the four of us?

I didn't bring it up right away because of the light, the moment, the warm hands, the glow. But I was thinking I would have to eventually. I'd have to ask Marnie again about her occupation, the occupation she scoffed at for the peach sex. The occupation the doctor and I knew very well, or at least could attest to as a cause for our strange actions. Our excuses. The whole set of evidence for Rex-occupation diminished and like two converging lines went away somewhere over there on the horizon.

No I wasn't going to bring it up. Ever.

It took all my will power to keep from fishing for her hand again to see if Rex was with us. And then, like a bird that squawks just before it takes off, as the light was going flat across the lake and the sky went pewter, I think we all saw the same thing because we all looked at each other at the same time.

It was a trick, of course. A good trick though. Somehow, and I go all the way out on the limb here, Rex made all three of our faces appear on the surface of the water like a momentary sharp image from a giant projector. Just our faces clearly and brightly filling the surface of the lake. We looked at each other to be sure the others had seen it too. Marnie just said, "Yes. I saw it."

The doctor sighed. "There are ways of explaining what we saw. The optics of water and sunset are notorious for creating illusions . . ." He trailed off. "I don't suppose anyone wants to hear the formula . . . no. I didn't think so." He bracketed the offer with another sigh.

Marnie smiled and said nothing. My crazy voice-hearing jealous-shit self wanted to speak at length, but didn't. Gin and tonic meds. But I couldn't help adding: "He just said goodbye, I think."

"I think he's over on the other porch being oracular now," Marnie said slowly. And we all laughed.

And then, as if to prove the show was still going to go on, all the light in the sky and on the lake became two notches brighter, and a large, single fish jumped in the exact middle of the water, and the ripples rolled out in perfect concentric circles.

Roundfire

FICTION

Put simply, we publish great stories. Whether it's literary or popular, a gentle tale or a pulsating thriller, the connecting theme in all Roundfire fiction titles is that once you pick them up you won't want to put them down.

If you have enjoyed this book, why not tell other readers by posting a review on your preferred book site. Recent bestsellers from Roundfire are:

The Bookseller's Sonnets

Andi Rosenthal

The Bookseller's Sonnets intertwines three love stories with a tale of religious identity and mystery spanning five hundred years and three countries.

Paperback: 978-1-84694-342-3 ebook: 978-184694-626-4

Birds of the Nile

An Egyptian Adventure

N.E. David

Ex-diplomat Michael Blake wanted a quiet birding trip up the Nile – he wasn't expecting a revolution.

Paperback: 978-1-78279-158-4 ebook: 978-1-78279-157-7

Blood Profit$

The Lithium Conspiracy

J. Victor Tomaszek, James N. Patrick, Sr.

The blood of the many for the profits of the few… *Blood Profit$* will take you into the cigar-smoke-filled room where American policy and laws are really made.

Paperback: 978-1-78279-483-7 ebook: 978-1-78279-277-2

The Burden

A Family Saga

N.E. David

Frank will do anything to keep his mother and father apart. But he's carrying baggage – and it might just weigh him down ...

Paperback: 978-1-78279-936-8 ebook: 978-1-78279-937-5

The Cause

Roderick Vincent

The second American Revolution will be a fire lit from an internal spark.

Paperback: 978-1-78279-763-0 ebook: 978-1-78279-762-3

Don't Drink and Fly

The Story of Bernice O'Hanlon: Part One

Cathie Devitt

Bernice is a witch living in Glasgow. She loses her way in her life and wanders off the beaten track looking for the garden of enlightenment.

Paperback: 978-1-78279-016-7 ebook: 978-1-78279-015-0

Gag

Melissa Unger

One rainy afternoon in a Brooklyn diner, Peter Howland punctures an egg with his fork. Repulsed, Peter pushes the plate away and never eats again.

Paperback: 978-1-78279-564-3 ebook: 978-1-78279-563-6

The Master Yeshua

The Undiscovered Gospel of Joseph

Joyce Luck

Jesus is not who you think he is. The year is 75 CE. Joseph ben Jude is frail and ailing, but he has a prophecy to fulfil ...

Paperback: 978-1-78279-974-0 ebook: 978-1-78279-975-7

On the Far Side, There's a Boy

Paula Coston

Martine Haslett, a thirty-something 1980s woman, plays hard on the fringes of the London drag club scene until one night which prompts her to sign up to a charity. She writes to a young Sri Lankan boy, with consequences far and long.

Paperback: 978-1-78279-574-2 ebook: 978-1-78279-573-5

Tuareg

Alberto Vazquez-Figueroa

With over 5 million copies sold worldwide, *Tuareg* is a classic adventure story from best-selling author Alberto Vazquez-Figueroa, about honour, revenge and a clash of cultures.

Paperback: 978-1-84694-192-4